LEGO NINJAGO

CHOOSE YOUR NINJA MISSION

WRITTEN BY SIMON HUGO

GET READY FOR A NINJA MISSION!

In this book, you are in charge of where your adventure leads. As you explore Ninjago Island and its surrounding realms, you'll find helpful ninja with useful vehicles but will also face some dangerous foes.

On every page, you will discover lots of incredible LEGO® NINJAGO® facts. Each choice you make will bring you closer to the end of your mission. But it won't always be a happy ending, so be sure to choose carefully!

When you reach the end of a mission, return to the start and begin again. You could retrace your steps and try to do things differently or try a completely new ninja path!

THE NINJA TEAM WILL HELP HOWEVER WE CAN!

YES! NEW MISSIONS ARE SO EXCITING!

WHERE WILL YOU GO FIRST?

Pick one of the two starting points below to start your own ninja mission. Good luck!

NINJA TRIAL

Nya invites you to test one of her new inventions. She doesn't give you many details, but promises it shouldn't be too dangerous and will help you prove your true potential to the ninja team. However, you also overhear her talking about ghosts, snake creatures, and a secretive biker gang. Do you dare accept the test?

TURN TO **1**

OR

TIME FOR TRAINING

Master Wu decides the time is right for you to study with him and learn to defeat some of the ninja's most powerful past enemies. The twinkle in his eye says that his history lessons won't all be taught in the dojo, though. That, and the fact that he tells you to prepare for sky, sand, and snow ... but first, you must make him a cup of tea.

TURN TO **2**

STEP INTO SIMJAGO!

Have you got what it takes to be a ninja? You may have wondered, and today you will get your answer! Nya the Water Ninja has invited you to try her latest creation: a virtual reality test chamber that she calls "Simjago." Complete one of its missions successfully and your reward will be ninja training with the real Master Wu! As Nya flicks the switch to start your test, the room around you seems to disappear and two new scenes replace it. Which will you step into?

FILE: PYTHOR

FILE: GENERAL KOZU

WU-GRU

FILE: PHANTOM NINJA

NYA KNOWS

As well as being the Elemental Master of Water, Nya is also a brilliant inventor. She builds many of the ninja's most impressive vehicles, and understands technology like few others. As the newest member of the ninja team, Nya also remembers what it's like to have to prove yourself!

WELCOME TO SIMJAGO!

Leap into the left-hand scene—where a super-fast flyer is speeding toward a spooky-looking city.

TURN TO **16**

OR

Walk toward the right-hand world, where something strange and snakelike is lurking in the bushes.

TURN TO **55**

You were only trying to be helpful when you made some tea for Master Wu. Unfortunately, you brewed his special Traveler's Tea and used a chronosteel teapot! Now the powerful pot is tumbling through time, and Wu needs you to get it back. He mixes a fresh cup of the special blend and stirs it with a chronosteel spoon. As soon as you drink it, you see time wind back before your tightly shut eyes. But when and where will you stop it to search for the missing teapot?

TEA FOR TRAVEL

Traveler's Tea is a very powerful drink, made with a secret recipe. Brewed properly, it allows the drinker to journey from one place to another in the blink of an eye. Chronosteel, meanwhile, is a very rare material that can harness the elemental power of Time. It is unwise for anyone but a Master to mix the two!

GET BACK BEFORE THE TEA COOLS!

Let the trail of the teapot guide you to a time when the ninja faced flying pirates!

TURN TO **13**

OR

Steer a course through time and space to investigate an island of snake-loving enemies!

TURN TO **41**

NINJA FACT!

Master Wu's peaceful tea room overlooks the training dojo where the ninja first learned the art of Spinjitzu.

TEAM SKYLOR

You distract the 'Condrai Copter long enough for Skylor to reach her flying rocket board and face her attackers. The commotion also draws the attention of Cole the Earth Ninja, who helps Skylor fend off the enemy in his own jet aircraft! What will you do now the danger is past?

DATA FILE

BOULDER BLASTER

» Nose cone is an eight-barrel rapid shooter

» Built by Cole, Zane, and Karlof the Elemental Master of Metal

» Also known as the Roto Jet

BOULDER BREAKOUT

Cole built his jet, the Boulder Blaster, in secret when he was captured by Master Chen during the Tournament of Elements. Cole enlisted the help of Chen's other captives, who were all being made to work in an underground noodle factory.

Rocket board

Take your quest into the sky with Cole. A bird's-eye view should help you find Wu's teapot!

TURN TO **104**

OR

Keep exploring on the ground with Skylor. This quest calls for close-up attention to detail!

TURN TO **102**

As soon as Jay makes the turn to the left, you see the mighty Morro Dragon, which is far larger than the beast you faced before! There is no time to waste as you ready the ghost-catching cannon on the back of the car and Jay gets the car into position. You fire off a shot and the dragon rears up in panic. It flies away and carries you off in its claws as it goes! Now what will you do?

GREEN WITH ENVY

The Morro Dragon is so named because the villainous Morro controls it. Before he became a ghost, Morro believed he was destined to be the Green Ninja, but he was badly mistaken. When he returns to Ninjago he steals Lloyd's elemental power to create his own twisted version of the ninja's green Energy Dragon.

Wriggle free from the dragon's clutches as it approaches the City of Stiix. It's not too far to fall!

TURN TO **119**

OR

Look on this as a chance to see somewhere new, and let the creature take you to its ghostly lair!

TURN TO **38**

NINJA FACT!

Morro cannot summon his own dragon without taking the Green Ninja's powers, because he has never conquered his own deepest fears.

NYA POWER!

The caves are dark and scary, and echo with a distant roaring sound. You are relieved when you find your way out into daylight—and to Nya the Water Ninja! You realize the sound you heard was Nya using her motorbike engine to recharge an old, abandoned pirate flyer. She says you can borrow one of the vehicles, but which one should you choose?

DATA FILE

NYA'S BIKE

» Adjustable elemental water cannon

» Golden water-bird design on front and sides

» Golden blades protect the front and back wheels

BRIDE AND DOOM

During the conflict with the Sky Pirates, Nya visits Tiger Widow Island to steal a sample of poison from its native giant spider. She knows this is the only thing that can defeat the pirate leader, Nadakhan. Unfortunately, Nadakhan desperately wants to marry Nya!

Nya's bike

Sky Pirate flyer

Borrow Nya's bike—after all, it is fit for a ninja! Perhaps Nya has also installed some secret weapons.

TURN TO **92**

OR

As you approach the wolf, you wonder if it might just want to eat you! But before you can turn back, it transforms into a friendly looking person! She says that her name is Akita, and that you must follow her to a nearby castle. You are too shocked to argue, but when you arrive you must decide what to do next …

LAST OF THE FORMLINGS

Akita belongs to a tribe called the Formlings, who have the ability to turn into animals. She is the only member of her village not to have been frozen solid by the Ice Emperor. Now she is on a solo mission to defeat her cold-hearted foe.

Now you're here, you might as well go into the castle and see why it's so important.

TURN TO **77**

OR

It could be a trap. Don't go in until you've taken the time to explore all around the castle.

TURN TO **80**

BUILD IT!

Use hinge bricks and other moving parts to build your own transforming creature. It could unfold from a wolf into a person, or from a bear into a bird!

IT'S NO YOLK!

As you crawl toward the nearest shell, you can't help brushing against the other eggs. The one with the crack in it topples over and breaks apart, revealing Kai the Fire Ninja! He had the same idea as you and has been hiding until the perfect moment to strike.

As he fights off the guard, you run deeper into the swamp and soon hear engines ahead. You can't turn back now, so what will you do?

I THINK IT'S TIME TO SCRAMBLE!

KAI'S SURPRISE

When the Vermillion first threaten Ninjago, it is Kai who uncovers their true role as servants of the Time Twins, Krux and Acronix. The Fire Ninja is shocked when he learns that his parents may also be in league with the Vermillion, and sets out to learn the truth, no matter how hard it is to hear.

Stay where you are and wait for Kai to catch up with you—assuming he won his battle!

TURN TO **46**

OR

Keep moving forward and see who is traveling through the swamp. It could be friend or foe!

TURN TO **43**

BUILD IT!

Snakes, ducks, frogs, and turtles all come from eggs. What other hatching creatures could you build, and what will their eggs look like?

You say goodbye to Jay and race off into the jungle on the Anacondrai vehicle. It's a fast machine, and its spinning blades cut a path through the undergrowth wherever you go. Unfortunately, this makes you easy to follow, and soon two identical vehicles are on your tail, with angry Anacondrai worshippers at the controls!

DATA FILE

ANACONDRAI CRUSHER

» Fires poisoned darts from its snakelike "mouth"

» Bats off rear attacks with a sharp, swiping tail

» Grips slippery surfaces with its studded wheels

Krait, the driver

SPIN CYCLES

'Condrai Crushers are the main mode of transport for the Anacondrai warriors. The Crushers get their name from the spinning stone blades on the front of each vehicle, which can be used to crush anything that gets in their way.

STOPPED IN YOUR TRACKS

The Anacondrai soldiers aren't happy that you've stolen their vehicle, and they use a remote control to bring you skidding to a halt. As their prisoner, you have time to reflect that stealing is never the answer!

» GO BACK AND TRY ANOTHER PATH!

When you reach the top of the tower, you see a hot-air balloon heading your way. You recognize the pilot as Master Wu, but he doesn't know you at all! You are confused for a moment, but then you remember: you are in the past, where Wu hasn't met you yet! He knows when someone needs help, however, so he offers to take you to one of his friends. But which one would you like to meet?

NEED A LIFT?

DATA FILE

HOT-AIR BALLOON

» Master Wu's personal flying machine

» Propeller-powered for speed and steering

» Room for two—or just for Wu!

Ask Master Wu to take you to Cole. The Earth Ninja is cool, calm, and good in a crisis.

TURN TO **24**

— OR —

Ask Wu to take you to Lloyd, the Green Ninja. His wisdom is second only to Master Wu's.

TURN TO **97**

WHO KNEW WU FLEW?

Master Wu doesn't often take to the skies, and when he does it's usually on a magnificent dragon! But Wu appreciates the simple things in life—such as this hot-air balloon. The craft isn't built for battle, but Wu keeps some coconut bombs stashed away in the basket in case of trouble!

The Pause Time Blade brings the Vermillion to a standstill, but also stops the river flowing—so the ninja's boat is stuck! Luckily, by the time the effects wear off, Jay the Lightning Ninja has arrived to supercharge the situation. The Vermillion can't compete with this amount of ninja force, so they have to flee. Now you need to choose which ninja to travel further into the swamp with …

DATA FILE

DESERT LIGHTNING
- » Started life as an everyday motorcycle
- » Designed for the desert but good to go anywhere!
- » Can be supercharged by Jay's elemental energy

RESHAPING THE PRESENT

Jay builds his bike out of a broken birthday gift when he visits his parents at their junkyard business. He goes there to protect the place from Vermillion attack after learning that the villains have started to steal scrap metal to make their vehicles and weapons of war.

Leave Lloyd and Cole on the boat and go with Jay on his motorbike to race after the retreating Vermillion.

TURN TO **66**

OR

Say thanks to Jay for his help, then stay on the boat with Lloyd and Cole to look for more Time Blades.

TURN TO **33**

BUILD IT!

Be like Jay and give a ninja twist to an ordinary vehicle. Build a car, a boat, or a plane, then fix it up with cool extras for an Elemental Master!

MISSION IMPOSSIBLE

There is little you can do as Princess Harumi uses the Oni Masks to summon up the ninja's greatest foe, Lord Garmadon! As the temple transforms around you and Garmadon appears with a fiery flash, you decide to try one last thing before you are destroyed! It seems completely impossible, but it might just work …

TWISTED TEMPLE

Ninjago's Royal Palace is also known as the Palace of Secrets, because of its many hidden tunnels and underground rooms. When it is reduced to ruins by the Sons of Garmadon, the Temple of Resurrection is revealed in full—as a horrifying shrine to darkness!

FLASH OF BRILLIANCE

Boom! Before you can carry out your brilliant idea (whatever it was!), you are pulled out of Simjago. By trying to do the impossible, you have reached a level of bravery the test could not compute, and so it has overloaded. Nya has no doubt that you are meant to be a ninja, and she can't wait to tell Master Wu!

>> CONGRATULATIONS! YOU HAVE COMPLETED YOUR NINJA MISSION!

RACE TO DANGER

As you race along the outskirts of the city on the back of Cole's Blaster Bike, you see frightened people running toward you. Cole comes to a halt and asks what is going on. Some folks are coming from the city center and say they are fleeing a phantom motorcycle. Others are approaching from the mountains and swear they have seen a gigantic ghost mech! You can only go one way, but which?

DATA FILE

BLASTER BIKE

» Twin fold-out, rapid-fire six-shooters

» Protective blades around the front and back wheels

» Cole's custom lavalike decals on the Deepstone bodywork

DEEPSTONE DRIVE

Inventor Cyrus Borg invented Cole's Blaster Bike as a way to combat Ghost Warriors. Its main body is made from purest Deepstone—a strange and rare material that saps spooks of their powers. Cole calls the bike his Ghost Cycle, but no ghost will ever get to ride it!

WHAT A BLAST!

Turn right into the city. Cole's bike is the perfect piece of gear for facing a supernatural cycle!

TURN TO 107

OR

Turn left into the mountains. Battling a giant ghost mech is the real ninja challenge here!

TURN TO 40

NINJA FACT!

Deepstone, the material used to make Cole's bike, is also ideal for making aeroblades—special weapons used for fighting ghosts!

BEACH BEGINNINGS

When you open your eyes, there is no sign of Master Wu or his dojo! You have been transported to a beautiful beach on a desert island. It is not entirely deserted, however: someone very large is running toward you! She is dressed like a pirate and doesn't look happy to see you. Should you say hello?

ORANGE CRUSH

This hulking brute is Dogshank, part of a ragtag band of scary Sky Pirates! When she was young she was granted three wishes, and asked to become a unique and remarkable-looking woman. The transformation did not go as she expected though! Since then, she has learned to love her powerful orange form.

HEY! THIS IS A PRIVATE BEACH!

No chance! Say your goodbyes instead and run away as fast as you can!

TURN TO **30**

OR

Why not? You have to take chances if you want to make friends in this new environment!

TURN TO **76**

BUILD IT!

Build a LEGO® beach using yellow plates for sand, small round pieces for rocks and shells, and white and transparent pieces for sea foam on the shore.

DESERT DROP

A sandstorm engulfs you as you fly into the desert realm, and you tumble to the ground with no idea where you are. You sense the shadow of a huge dragon flying overhead, before you pass out in the sand. When you awake, the storm has passed, and a huge vehicle is thundering your way. How will you react?

DATA FILE

DIESELNAUT

» All-terrain battle tank

» Multiple missile launchers

» The fiercest ride in the First Realm!

FIRST PLACE

This sandy place is the First Realm, also known as the Realm of Oni and Dragons. The oldest of all realms, it was once home to the First Spinjitzu Master, who created Ninjago Island. Now the only beings who live here are ancient dragons and villainous Dragon Hunters.

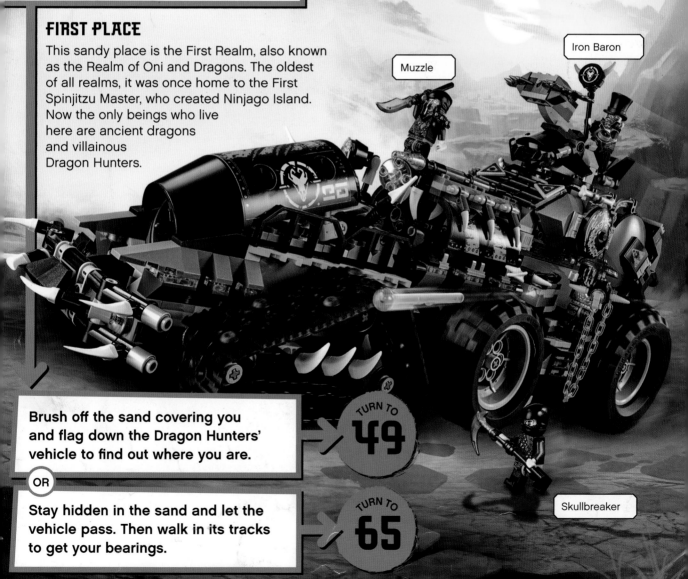

Muzzle

Iron Baron

Skullbreaker

Brush off the sand covering you and flag down the Dragon Hunters' vehicle to find out where you are.

TURN TO 49

OR

Stay hidden in the sand and let the vehicle pass. Then walk in its tracks to get your bearings.

TURN TO 65

WALK, DON'T RUN!

Rushing deep into the temple to get far away from the guard, you run straight into the familiar figure of Master Chen. He invited the ninja to the island. You recognize his smiling face from the logo of his restaurant chain, Chen's Noodle House. But for some reason he isn't smiling now!

MASTER OF WAR

Long ago, Master Chen was banished to a remote island as punishment for starting a war on Ninjago Island. During his exile, he plotted a revenge that would destroy Ninjago City, but also opened a popular noodle restaurant there!

REVENGE IS A DISH BEST SERVED WITH NOODLES!

Master Chen

CAUGHT BY THE CULT

Master Chen yells for his guards and suddenly you are surrounded by tough-looking soldiers! You know the Anacondrai's plans will soon be foiled by the ninja, but on this occasion, they have defeated you!

>> GO BACK AND TRY ANOTHER PATH!

You begin your mission as a passenger on board the R.E.X.—a fast and powerful flying machine belonging to the bounty hunter Ronin. As he pilots the craft, you ask Ronin to remind you where you are going. He laughs and says you are heading for the City of Stiix, of course! Unless there is somewhere safer where you would rather go. Is there?

DATA FILE

R.E.X.

» Twin blasters protect cargo stored behind cockpit

» It can also function as a submarine

» R.E.X. initials don't stand for anything!

FRIEND OR FOE?

Ronin used to be a bad guy, but when he got to know the ninja he decided to change his ways. He has helped them battle the Ghost Warriors, the Sky Pirates, the Vermillion, and the Sons of Garmadon, with his reliable R.E.X. proving useful on more than one occasion.

There's nowhere you'd rather see than Stiix, which is famous for its lively criminal underworld!

TURN TO 119

OR

The City of Stiix does not sound like your kind of place! Ask Ronin to take you to see the ninja instead.

TURN TO 87

NINJA VICTORY

Of course your ninja ally didn't need your help to defeat his opponent! After winning the battle, he introduces you to the other ninja and their friend Samurai X. The whole gang is eager to celebrate the impressive victory at the ninjas' mobile base. Will you accept an invitation to the party?

Samurai X glider

Jay's Electromech

Lloyd's Jungle Raider

THE X FACTOR

Before she becomes a ninja, Nya is the mysterious Samurai X. For a time Nya wore the disguise to have her own secret adventures, but by the time of the Tournament of Elements Samurai X works alongside the ninja, who all know her true identity.

Yes—there's always time for a party! And perhaps the missing teapot is at the ninja's base ...

TURN TO
105

OR

No—Wu didn't send you here to have fun! Go and search the rest of the tournament alone.

TURN TO
88

NINJA FACT!

While the other ninja compete in the Tournament of Elements, Zane the Ice Ninja is a prisoner of Master Chen.

When it sees the R.E.X. speeding toward it, the ghost dragon takes fright and disappears like a ghost! The Skreemers follow suit, and the ninja are safe, thanks to you! They invite you on board *Destiny's Bounty*, where they tell you about the missions they are planning. Your help could be valuable to them once again, but which mission should you go on?

DATA FILE

DESTINY'S BOUNTY 2.0

» Cannons on both sides of the ship

» Retractable rotating harpoon shooter

» Space to stow a flying motorbike in the back

Go with Jay the Lightning Ninja to investigate ghost sightings in the heart of Ninjago City.

TURN TO 81

OR

Go with Cole the Earth Ninja to check out ghostly goings-on where the city meets the mountains.

TURN TO 12

BONUS BOUNTY

This is the second flying ship to bear the name *Destiny's Bounty.* Nya and Master Wu designed this all-new, tech-filled replacement for their first airborne base. They have kept the style of the previous ancient sailing ship, so it still feels like home to the ninja!

FLIGHT INTO DANGER

Lloyd laughs when you tell him about your experience on the island and agrees to take you back and face the danger. But when you arrive he doesn't even get a chance to land, as two pirates launch an attack from the sky. Lloyd's dragon is far more powerful that the pirates' small flyer, so they quickly turn and flee. But what made them attack in the first place?

DATA FILE

PIRATE FLYER
» Nose is a six-barrel rapid shooter
» Flag displays the symbol of the Sky Pirates
» Flagpole for a passenger to cling on to!

Monkey Wretch

PEW! PEW!

SINGING AND SWINGING
The pilot of the pirate flyer is Cyren, whose singing voice can send her enemies into a trance! Her companion is Monkey Wretch. He was once a human being, but Nadakhan, the captain of the Sky Pirates, turned him into a mechanical monkey who swings from the sails of the pirates' ships!

Cyren

They must have been guarding something important on the island! Stick around and take a look.

TURN TO
28

OR

They were determined to be somewhere else in a hurry. Chasing after them is the thing to do!

TURN TO
59

BUILD IT!

Try building a seafaring ship for the Sky Pirates in case they want to swap flying for sailing. Mimic their signature style, using brown and orange pieces.

Zane goes to retrieve the mask while you speed after the escaping bikers. But after a few sharp twists and turns you start to wonder if they are taking you for a ride! When you move in closer, you see that the lead biker is wearing another Oni Mask. You are caught off guard as the gang surround you, and you realize that the first mask was just a decoy to get rid of Zane and lure you into a trap!

DATA FILE

ONI BIKE

» Ridden by Nindroid biker Mr. E

» Equipped with giant, foldaway chopping blades

» Flies the flag of the Sons of Garmadon

Luke Cunningham

Mr. E, with Oni Mask powers

DEMONIC DRESS-UP

The three Oni Masks were created by demons called the Oni long before Ninjago existed. Each has its own powers—such as the red Mask of Vengeance, which turns the wearer into a four-armed master sword fighter—and the Sons of Garmadon want to steal them all!

HIGH-PERFORMANCE RACER

Back in the real world, the real Zane has joined Nya and is impressed by your Simjago performance, even though you ended up in a trap! Both ninja agree you have enough potential to be given another chance!

» GO BACK AND TRY ANOTHER PATH!

JAILBIRD JAY

By the time you catch up with Jay he has been locked up in a spooky cell! It is suspended from an enchanted chain, so there is no way for you to reach him on your own. You look around for someone who can help you mount a rescue. Through the chaos of the ongoing battle, you see two possible aids. Who should you turn to?

LEADING AND LEARNING

While in the City of Stiix, Jay briefly becomes the ninja's leader. It is not a role he really wants, however, as he prefers to be an equal partner within the team. Around this time, Jay and the other ninja also learn the ancient martial art of Airjitzu—or, as Jay likes to call it, "Cyclon-do"!

THE ONLY LOCKS I LIKE ARE LIGHTNING BOLTS!

Go over to a nearby tea trader. He may not be a trained ninja, but at least he seems to have found a spot clear of the fighting!

TURN TO **61**

OR

Step into the battle, where a gaggle of ghosts is all that separates you from Lloyd the Green Ninja.

TURN TO **60**

NINJA FACT!

Only a prison built with powerful Vengestone is strong enough to trap an Elemental Master like Jay the Lightning Ninja!

After several hours flying around the First Realm, you conclude that yes—it is nothing but desert! There is certainly no sign of Wu's missing teapot. In fact, you and your low-flying dragon are the only distinctive features in the desolate landscape. You soon attract the attention of a pair of Dragon Hunters in a fast and fully armed chopper!

DATA FILE

HUNTERCOPTER

» Dragon Hunters' aerial attack craft

» Armed with anti-dragon shooters and a Vengestone chain

» Stocked with turkey legs to use as dragon bait

TO CATCH A DRAGON

How does a simple helicopter catch a huge Elemental Dragon? By carrying weapons and chains made out of Vengestone—a substance that can stop elemental powers from working! The Dragon Hunters use it to ensnare and imprison their prey—be it a dragon or an Elemental Master!

Muzzle

Heavy Metal

CHOPPER STOPPER

After hours of flying, even a mighty dragon can't escape a HunterCopter. The creature is easily captured by the Dragon Hunters, and you are their bonus prize! If only you'd left this realm when you had the chance …

>> GO BACK AND TRY ANOTHER PATH!

OVER AND OUT

You try to destroy the mask, but when you slam it against the road it pulses with an energy that knocks you over and out cold! When you come around you are not sure how much time has passed, but the mask is gone and the biker gang is running the city. Nobody dares challenge the bikers' rule, because they are backed up by a massive monster. If only this were a bad dream …

MONSTER OF ROCK

The huge stone monster is called the Colossus (or the Oni Titan). It was created by Lord Garmadon as a show of strength, after the Sons of Garmadon succeed in bringing him back from the Departed Realm.

THE REAL DEAL

With the test at an end, Simjago disappears as if it were just a dream. But Nya says it was more than a fantasy, because you learned an important lesson about being a ninja: never rely on brute force alone!

>> GO BACK AND TRY ANOTHER PATH!

IS IT A BIRD?

You speed away from the island, looking for Cole. Traveling high above the ocean, you see a large bird in the distance. But as it gets closer you realize it is not a bird at all—it is Cole riding an Elemental Earth Dragon! He flies alongside Wu's balloon and you make the daring jump to the dragon's back. Cole says he is on a mission to thwart some Sky Pirates. Are you willing to help him?

GOOD LUCK, NINJA!

FEARLESS FLYERS

Just like the other ninja, Cole can make his Elemental Dragon appear by overcoming his fears. If his fear gets the better of him, the dragon will disappear! The ninja refer to their hard-learned ability to control their emotions as "dragon power."

SORRY, THERE ARE NO SEAT BELTS!

Elemental Earth Dragon

Yes—wherever he's heading has to be better than where you've already been!

TURN TO
37

OR

Yes—and you know exactly where he should go to find one very big, scary pirate!

TURN TO
36

NINJA FACT!

When the ninja first encounter the Sky Pirates, Cole is technically a living ghost who can turn himself invisible!

HOT WHEELS

You run for cover behind a row of cars, but Fire Fang sends them scattering with its tail. For a moment you are totally exposed, but then another, bigger car pulls up. It's Kai the Fire Ninja in a mighty 4x4! He says one vehicle is no match for Fire Fang. So who should he call for back up?

DATA FILE

KATANA 4X4

» Forward-mounted shuriken slicer weapon

» Missile launchers hidden in front grille

» Turbo-boosters for extra speed

ALL-TERRAIN ACTION

Kai's Katana 4x4 is built for use in the Desert of Doom, but its big balloon tires can take it anywhere. The ninja go to the desert to explore an ancient pyramid, only to find that the villain Aspheera had been trapped inside it for a thousand years. When she gets free, her first stop is Ninjago City!

Call on Cole the Earth Ninja, with his golden hammer and armored dirt bike.

TURN TO 50

OR

Tap up Titanium Ninja Zane, who is always ice cool and has his own helicopter.

TURN TO 94

A TIMELESS APPROACH

Realizing that it is too dangerous to use the blade near Iron Doom, you resort to some trickery! Pretending to use the Pause Time Blade on yourself and the ninja by accident, you stand stock still while the Time Twins laugh at your foolishness. Only when their guard is down do you leap into action, bringing Iron Doom down with good old-fashioned ninja weapons. They are truly timeless!

TWINS REUNITED

Time Twins Acronix and Krux were separated for 40 years while Acronix was lost in time. When Acronix returns to Ninjago, he has not aged a day, while Krux has become old and gray. The one thing the pair still have in common is their desire to make Ninjago pay for all the time they have spent apart!

VIRTUAL VICTORY

With Iron Doom defeated, your challenge is over. Nya says your tactics could only have worked in Simjago—but as understanding your environment is key to being a ninja, you must have passed the test!

>> CONGRATULATIONS! YOU HAVE COMPLETED YOUR NINJA MISSION!

KAI VERSUS KARLOF

You arrive at the tournament in time to see Kai doing battle with Karlof, the Elemental Master of Metal. Lloyd advises you not to interfere in their duel, and heads off on a mission of his own. But as you watch the fight, it really looks as if Kai might lose. Should you step in after all?

HEAVY METAL

With his ability to turn himself into solid metal, Karlof makes a formidable opponent at the Tournament of Elements. But while he can be steely and hard-headed, he has a heart of gold and eventually becomes a cast-iron ally of the ninja.

TAKE THAT!

YOU TAKE THAT BACK!

No—Lloyd knows best! Follow the Green Ninja's advice and resist your urge to help Kai.

TURN TO **17**

OR

Yes—if Lloyd could see the duel now, he would surely want you to step in to help.

TURN TO **109**

NINJA FACT!

There are many Elemental Masters besides the ninja. Each one has harnessed the power of the world around them.

When you tell Lloyd you want to explore the island, he lands just long enough for you to leap down from the dragon. He wishes you luck before taking off again to chase the fleeing Sky Pirates on his own. You comb the beach from end to end, but find nothing unusual—just one solitary Sky Pirate who has been left behind to clear up after the others!

SWEEPING DUTIES

Serpentine Sky Pirate Clancee is the lowliest member of Nadakhan's crew. He always wanted to be a pirate, but he gets seasick and airsick so spends most of his time sweeping instead of swashbuckling! He is very loyal to his fellow Sky Pirates, as they are the closest thing to family he has ever had.

LET'S GET THIS BEACH SHIPSHAPE!

BROOM AND BUST

This island holds no more mysteries—and certainly not any time-traveling teapots! Coming back here was a mistake, and now all you can do to make yourself useful is pick up a broom and help to keep the beach tidy!

>> GO BACK AND TRY ANOTHER PATH!

THE FACE OF HATRED

As soon as you get your hands on the Oni Mask, the biker gang speeds out of sight. Your ninja companion roars off after the gang, leaving you to deal with the fearsome face! You can feel the dangerous energy flowing through it, and are not even slightly tempted to try it on. But what will you do with it instead?

PURPLE POWERS

The three Oni Masks are the red Mask of Vengeance, the orange Mask of Deception, and the purple Mask of Hatred. All of them grant a special, dark power to the wearer. The purple mask turns the wearer's body into molten rock, making them almost invincible!

Mask of Hatred

Take the mask to the safety of the Royal Palace. It is one of the most highly guarded places in the city.

TURN TO
51

OR

The mask may be too powerful to be safely stored anywhere. Destroy it here, while you can.

TURN TO
23

NINJA FACT!

For many years, the Mask of Hatred was hidden behind two giant waterfalls in the jungle lands known as Primeval's Eye.

UPS AND DOWNS

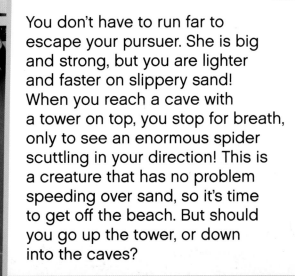

You don't have to run far to escape your pursuer. She is big and strong, but you are lighter and faster on slippery sand! When you reach a cave with a tower on top, you stop for breath, only to see an enormous spider scuttling in your direction! This is a creature that has no problem speeding over sand, so it's time to get off the beach. But should you go up the tower, or down into the caves?

Venomous spider

Go up! You can see the whole island and plan your next move from there.

TURN TO 9

OR

Go down! Long, winding caves might take you much further than the tower.

TURN TO 5

SECRET SPIDER

The massive Tiger Widow spider is found in just one place: Tiger Widow Island! This isolated isle is almost unknown in modern Ninjago, but the buildings suggest that someone lived there long ago. Today, the ninja and the Sky Pirates are the only ones who know that the island—and the spider—exist at all!

You are so busy concentrating on doing nothing that you forget to hold on tight! An unexpected sharp turn as you approach the base causes you to tumble out of your seat and straight into the pirates' lair! Facing lone pirates was bad enough, but now you're surrounded by a whole horrible crew of them!

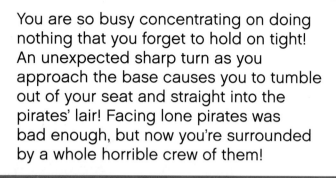

Bucko

Flintlocke

Cyren

Clancee

WELL, SHIVER ME TIMBERS, WHAT HAVE WE HERE?

MISSING IN ACTION

You look up to see what caused the sudden swerve and see all the ninja on their dragons doing battle with a fleet of Sky Pirate ships! In all the excitement, your escort hasn't even noticed you're gone, so you're stuck as a prisoner on the pirate base!

》GO BACK AND TRY ANOTHER PATH!

Running fast, you don't look back until you reach a river. When you see a ninja boat coming your way, you jump on board—only to realize that you've leapt straight into a battle with the Vermillion! Lloyd the Green Ninja asks you to take the boat's controls as he fends off an attack. You do so just in time to see four strange missiles heading for the deck. Which way will you steer to dodge them?

DATA FILE

DESTINY'S SHADOW

» Designed to operate in air, in water, and even on land

» Smart systems include collision-avoidance technology

» Equipped with quiet canoes for stealth swamp missions

BIRTHDAY BOAT

Lloyd's mother gave him his own boat for his birthday. *Destiny's Shadow* may be much smaller than the ninja's main ship, *Destiny's Bounty*, but it can fly just like the larger vessel thanks to its fold-out wings. It even has a mini fridge for refreshing post-battle beverages!

Slackjaw

Rivett

Vermin

Hard-a-port—otherwise known to landlubbers as taking a sharp left!

TURN TO 84

OR

Hard-a-starboard—or what non-sailors might call right here, right now!

TURN TO 39

BUILD IT!

What would a water vessel for the Vermillion look like? Play around with red and gray bricks to make a snakelike boat or submarine!

You search the water where the other two blades must have splashed down, but can find only one—the Reversal Time Blade. The Vermillion must have escaped with the Forward Time Blade, which is bad news for everyone! You would normally chase after a villain, but you're holding a time blade ... perhaps you can change history so the villains never got the blade to begin with?

A BLAST FROM THE PAST

The Reversal Time Blade has many different powers. As well as letting the wearer travel back into the past, it can also be used to make time go backward for other people, and even to make people younger. This last ability is especially useful if someone has been made to age quickly using the Forward Time Blade!

Reversal Time Blade

Give chase. If you rewind time, events could play out the same all over again—or maybe even worse!

TURN TO
66

OR

The Vermillion are long gone. Use the blade to travel back in time to before you boarded the boat.

TURN TO
32

NINJA FACT!

The Reversal Time Blade spent many years at the bottom of the Boiling Sea, where it was safe from the Time Twins.

PLANE TO SEE

When you ask to meet a ninja, young Master Wu raises his arms and signals into the sky. Moments later, a sleek one-seater jet touches down on the smooth, compacted sand and Kai the Fire Ninja jumps out. When you explain your important mission, Kai insists that you borrow his jet, and he and Wu wave you off as you take off for a bird's-eye teapot search!

DATA FILE

DESTINY'S WING

» Missile launchers under each wing

» Projectile weapons on top of each wing

» Katana blades stored on each side of cockpit

WHO ORDERED HOT WINGS?

BUILT FROM THE *BOUNTY*

The Dragon Hunters built *Destiny's Wing* from the stolen wreckage of the ninja's ship, *Destiny's Bounty 2.0*. Later, the ninja claim the aircraft back as their own and use it to escape from the hunters' leader, Iron Baron.

WINGING IT

Flying low to spot every detail, you search for hours before deciding there is nothing to see! Without a single landmark to guide you back to Kai and Wu, you are now well and truly lost in this barren realm.

>> GO BACK AND TRY ANOTHER PATH!

You dash after the bikers and see that they are taking the highway to central Ninjago City. It runs directly alongside the canal. You are not the only one following them! Lloyd has been waiting for them in his car, while Kai is coming alongside them in a boat on the canal. Who should you team up with?

URBAN SPRAWL

Ninjago City is a sprawling, multi-layered mass of crisscrossing bridges, canals, and skyways. In fact, it sometimes feels more like a maze than a place to live! One way to find your way around is to remember that the oldest buildings are found on the lower levels, while the newest ones soar high above them. They have simply been built over the top!

Luke Cunningham

NO NINJA IS FAST ENOUGH TO CATCH US!

Skip Vicious

Leap into the passenger seat of Lloyd's car. He will have no trouble keeping up with this mysterious biker gang.

TURN TO **64**

OR

Jump on board the boat with Kai. He should have more luck staying out of sight as he follows the gang on water.

TURN TO **96**

NINJA FACT!

Gang members Luke Cunningham and Skip Vicious look very similar in their biker helmets, but underneath they have different hair.

SHARK ATTACK!

When Cole hears about your experience on the island, he recognizes Dogshank from your description and speeds you back there on his dragon. But when you arrive, you see that Dogshank is no longer on her own. She has been joined by fellow pirate Flintlocke in his sleek and powerful Sky Shark. Together they are more than a match for one small dragon!

DATA FILE

SKY SHARK

» Smothered in swords, pistols, and blunderbuss guns!

» Treasure chest compartments built into both wings

» Designed to drop dynamite— or rotten fish!

NADAKHAN'S NUMBER ONE

Flintlocke used to be a pirate captain himself, but he accidentally sank his own ship! Now he is the Sky Pirates' second in command, serving under Nadakhan. Other members of Nadakhan's crew look to him for guidance when they are too scared to talk to their leader!

Flintlocke

DOWN TO EARTH

Cole does his best to fight off the Sky Shark, but his dragon is quickly exhausted and has to land. As the Sky Pirates gleefully take you captive, you ask yourself: whatever made you come back to this island?

>> GO BACK AND TRY ANOTHER PATH!

TO THE LIGHTHOUSE!

As you soar across the ocean, you wonder where you are headed—until you see an ancient lighthouse where Sky Pirates and ninja are doing battle. When you swoop down to land in the heart of the action, you realize you are the reinforcements! But you haven't come here looking for a fight—you're looking for a special teapot! Is it possible that you've just found it?

ECHO FROM THE PAST

This lighthouse was once used by the fearsome Skeleton Army to imprison Dr. Julien—the father of Zane the Ice Ninja. Now, years later, as the ninja battle the pirates, they discover another of Julien's "children"—a friendly clockwork robot called Echo Zane!

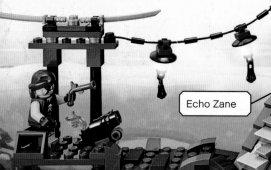

Echo Zane

Sqiffy

I WILL PROTECT YOU, NINJA!

Yes! There's Master Wu's teapot above the mailbox. Grab it now and ignore the fighting!

TURN TO **82**

OR

No! That teapot must be a trap to keep you from helping the ninja. Ignore it and go into battle!

TURN TO **111**

BUILD IT!

Why not make some catapults and missile launchers for the pirates, or a fighter craft so the ninja can make an aerial attack from the lighthouse?

Bad idea! Before you know it, you are overwhelmed by ghostly forces flying at you from all sides! Skreemers, ghost dragons, and Ghost Warriors are everywhere you look, and—because you can see through them—you can also see even more monsters bringing up the rear! Being bold in the face of danger is all well and good, but you realize that this time you have been careless, not courageous!

GHOUL SCHOOL

Morro's Ghost Warriors come in different shapes and sizes, but all originate from the Cursed Realm. They have the power to possess people and objects to make them do their bidding, and can even turn people into ghosts for good! Escaped ghosts can be sent back to the Cursed Realm or to rest in peace in the Departed Realm.

Ghost Ninja Attila

Chain Master Wrayth

Scythe Master Ghoultar

DANGER WARNING

As the simulation ends, Nya's sympathetic face replaces the grinning ghouls. She says that being a ninja isn't about diving headlong into danger—it's about picking the right risks and being wise to the wrong ones!

>> GO BACK AND TRY ANOTHER PATH!

A QUESTION OF TIME

For all your efforts, you can't stop two of the missiles landing on the boat. But when you go to take a closer look, you see that they aren't missiles at all but a pair of powerful Time Blades! With the Vermillion still attacking the boat, you wonder: which blade should you use to save the day?

LOST AND FOUND

Forged from chronosteel, the four Time Blades are so powerful that they must never be combined! They were made to strip the elemental powers from the evil Time Twins and then deliberately scattered and lost in time. When they are found again, the Twins can't wait to become the Elemental Masters of Time once more!

Pause Time Blade

Slow-Mo Time Blade

Use the red Pause Time Blade to put the battle on hold until ninja reinforcements can arrive.

TURN TO
10

OR

Use the blue Slow-Mo Time Blade to make the Vermillion move more like snails than snakes!

TURN TO
117

BUILD IT!

Master your own time by creating a LEGO clock! Build a numbered clock face, then add hands you can set to show things like lunch and dinner time.

Making your way into the mountains, you soon catch sight of the huge ghost mech that had everyone so scared! You are looking for a true ninja challenge, but Cole knows it would be foolish to tackle this foe without help. He says you must always pick your battles wisely. Is this really the right mission for you?

DATA FILE

MECH-ENSTEIN

» Wields four enormous ghost swords

» Piloted by Blade Master Bansha

» Open cockpit, with pilot held in place by bones

EX-SAMURAI MECH

The ghost mech used to be a red robot walker belonging to Samurai X. It is possessed by the spectral power of Scythe Master Ghoultar when the Ghost Warriors invade the Samurai X Cave. From this point on, it turns a ghoulish green and goes by the name of Mech-enstein!

WHO ARE YOU GOING TO CALL, NINJA?

Yes it is! All you need is backup. Send for Zane the Titanium Ninja and his own mighty mech.

TURN TO 118

OR

No—you need an even bigger challenge! Call out for Nya to set Simjago to its toughest level.

TURN TO 112

NINJA FACT!

The Ghost Warriors use their stolen mech to climb the Wailing Alps (Ninjago's tallest mountain range), and reach a portal to another Realm.

THE ADVENTURE BEGINS

When you open your eyes, you are no longer in Master Wu's dojo. The sounds, smells, and heat of the jungle surround you, and a huge serpent's head is looming over you! A split second of fear passes as you realize the head is part of an ancient stone temple. What should you do first?

REPTILE HOUSE

Temples like this one are used by Anacondrai worshippers. They want to turn themselves into snakelike creatures, but need elemental powers to do so. To achieve this, they invite the ninja to a Tournament of Elements on a jungle island and try to steal their abilities!

IS THERE SOMEONE THERE?

Anacondrai worshipper, Zugu

That snake's head is scary! Explore the jungle around the temple before going inside.

TURN TO 62

OR

The jungle looks even scarier! Go into the temple and look for Master Wu's missing teapot.

TURN TO 74

BUILD IT!

Think of your favorite animal and make a ninja base inspired by it, or think of a creature that scares you and build a villains' lair that looks like it!

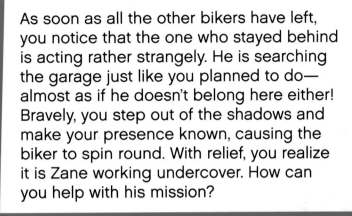

As soon as all the other bikers have left, you notice that the one who stayed behind is acting rather strangely. He is searching the garage just like you planned to do—almost as if he doesn't belong here either! Bravely, you step out of the shadows and make your presence known, causing the biker to spin round. With relief, you realize it is Zane working undercover. How can you help with his mission?

INTRUDER DETECTED ... AND I DON'T MEAN ME.

ZANE BY ANOTHER NAME

When Zane goes undercover, he uses his Nindroid holographic systems to disguise himself. They also allow him to change back to his normal appearance in the blink of an eye. Whenever Zane is in his biker disguise, he uses the name "Snake Jaguar," which Cole invented for him.

Help Zane find what he is looking for—a powerful Oni Mask that the bikers have stolen.

TURN TO **57**

OR

Leave Zane to search while you pass a coded message to his undercover contact, Samurai X.

TURN TO **99**

X ON THE SPOT

You push through the swamp until you see Samurai X speeding past with Vermillion vehicles on her tail! You wave, and the villains are distracted long enough for her to blast them with her cannons and for you to leap into her car. She says she is heading for an abandoned enemy base. Samurai X is concentrating on driving, so asks you to come up with a plan for when you get there.

DATA FILE

SAMURAI VXL

» A gift from Nya to the new Samurai X

» Armed with two rapid-fire six-shooters

» Used to be red until P.I.X.A.L. turned it blue

PUTTING THE "X" IN P.I.X.A.L.

When the ninja face the Vermillion, they are helped by the second Samurai X. Not even Nya (the original Samurai X) knows who the newcomer is, but later on they learn that she is their old friend P.I.X.A.L. in a brand new android body!

Search one half of the base while Samurai X searches the other. It's the fastest way!

TURN TO **78**

OR

Search the entire base together. It will take longer, but you might feel safer as a team!

TURN TO **101**

NINJA FACT!

The android P.I.X.A.L. was built by the scientist Cyrus Borg. Her name stands for "Primary Interactive X-ternal Assistant Life-form."

The tea on the table is still warm when the pair who made it come out from the cupboard where they have been hiding. They introduce themselves as Ray and Maya—Kai and Nya's long-lost parents! Though their home looks like a nice place, it has been their prison for many years. But now you have found them, they can escape and be reunited with their family once again!

FROM MASTERS TO SLAVES

Long before Kai and Nya became ninja, Ray was the Elemental Master of Fire and Maya was the Master of Water. After their powers passed on to their children, the couple were captured by the Time Twins, who forced them to stay in a swampland home and make armor for the Vermillion!

Ray

Maya

ANOTHER TOP-UP? YES PLEASE!

NINJA FACT!

The Time Twins have a grudge against Ray and Maya because they once made four special Time Blades to strip them of their powers.

FRIEND OF THE FAMILY

Nya's beaming face is the first thing you see as the simulation ends. She says you have passed the test by making new friends instead of enemies—and yes, her parents are now safe and well!

>> CONGRATULATIONS! YOU HAVE COMPLETED YOUR NINJA MISSION!

INTO THE FIRE

In the blink of an eye your dragon transports you out of the First Realm and into the heart of Ninjago City. You guide the creature in to land, but a jet of flame blasts you off its back as you touch down. When the dragon flees in fear, you look up from where you have fallen and see a huge, fire-breathing snake! What would a ninja do now?

BURN NINJAGO, BURN!

Aspheera

GROWN FROM LAVA

This flame-tongued terror is Fire Fang— sorceress Aspheera's favorite mode of transportation. She conjured the creature out of lava, and now she and her army of Pyro Vipers use it to wreak havoc in Ninjago City!

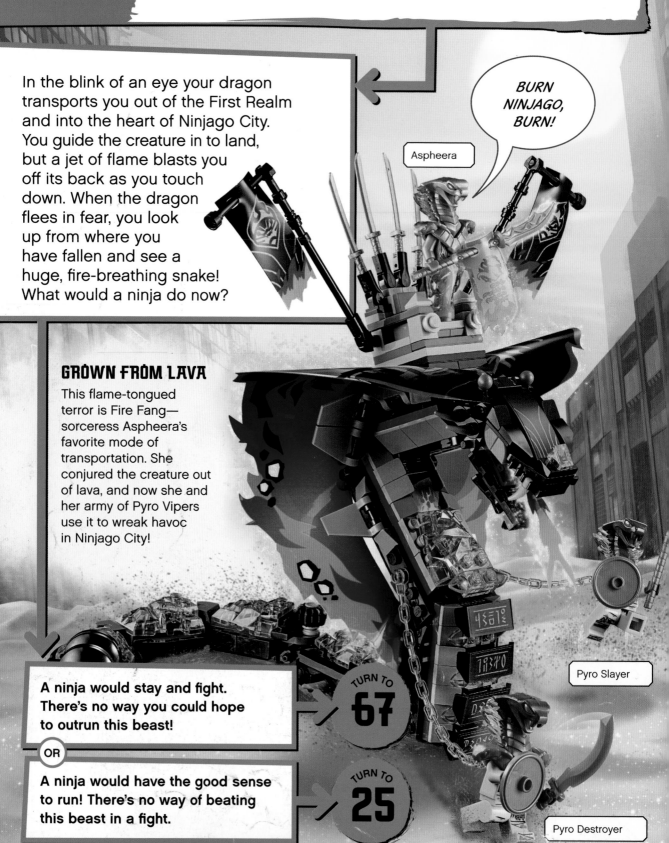

Pyro Slayer

Pyro Destroyer

A ninja would stay and fight. There's no way you could hope to outrun this beast!

TURN TO 67

OR

A ninja would have the good sense to run! There's no way of beating this beast in a fight.

TURN TO 25

Staying still in a swamp is never a good idea! You immediately start to sink in the mud, and as the engine noise gets louder you realize it is heading your way! Unable to move, you can only watch as a huge Vermillion vehicle plows its way through the plant life and the pilot claims you as his muddy prisoner. As the craft carries on with you on board, you look back to see Kai arriving just too late to help!

DATA FILE

VERMILLION INVADER

» Fires eggs to shower enemies with snakes

» Central tank tread can crawl over any obstacle

» Pincerlike prongs fend off forward attacks

SNAKES THAT TAKE

The Vermillion steal scrap metal from Ninjago City to build up their fleet of vehicles. They kidnap builders and mechanics and force them to make machines to their distinctive designs—which often include tank-tread wheels for slithering along like a snake!

Commander Raggmunk

STANDING ORDERS

As the simulation fades, you realize you are not really covered in mud at all! But that is the only good news, as Nya says you have not passed the test this time. A true ninja never stands still for long, she tells you!

» GO BACK AND TRY ANOTHER PATH!

NO HANDS ON DECK

You were right—the ship is so solid that you and Samurai X are able to jump aboard, ready to battle the crew. But when you get on deck, you see that this creepy craft has no crew! As Samurai X returns to her speedboat, you take the wheel of the ship and sail into the City of Stiix as if you were just another ghost. From here, you can see a battle is underway. So what should you do next?

DATA FILE

GHOST SHIP

» Can float on water—or in the sky!

» Has a jail cell for non-spook stowaways

» Wind passes right through the ragged sail!

BAY OF DISMAY

As a port city, Stiix is often home to unusual ships. A green-glowing ghost vessel might stand out in some places, but not in a harbor that also plays host to Ronin's flying R.E.X. submarine; the ninja's *Destiny's Bounty*; and the Sky Pirates' mighty vessel, the *Misfortune's Keep*!

It looks like the ninja are at the heart of the battle. Speed toward a red blur that looks like Kai the Fire Ninja.

TURN TO **106**

OR

One ninja is surrounded by so many ghosts you can barely see him! Fight your way to Lloyd the Green Ninja.

TURN TO **60**

JAY BREAK!

When you sneak up to the cell, you realize the prisoner inside is the Lightning Ninja, Jay! With your help Jay is soon free, and he is grateful for your assistance. He offers to take you away from the jungle in his mech, which is hidden nearby, but you have spotted an unattended Anacondrai vehicle that you could pilot yourself. What will you do?

SOLITARY CONFINEMENT

It's not easy to trap lightning! Master Chen pits the ninja against each other in the tournament so they are not able to work as a team. It's the only way for Chen to stand a chance of capturing the ninja and stealing their powers.

> QUICK, LET'S GET OUT OF HERE!

Make a speedy getaway with the Ninja of Lightning to find out what lies beyond the jungle.

TURN TO 116

OR

Use the Anacondrai vehicle to go undercover and stay and explore the jungle on your own.

TURN TO 8

BUILD IT!

This prison cell has doors made from bones! What unusual pieces in your LEGO collection could combine to make a ninja trap or jail?

SNARED IN THE SAND

As the vehicle gets closer, you see it is crawling with scary-looking characters. You start to wish you hadn't given it a wave, but it's too late now—they have seen you! Before you can say hello, a pair of villains leap down to grab you, then bundle you into their on-board jail cell. Now what are you going to do?

MEET THE HUNTERS

These masked villains are the Dragon Hunters—a hard-bitten bunch of desert dwellers who survive by catching elemental creatures. If a dragon is unlucky enough to fall into the Hunters' clutches, it will be made to fight for their amusement, used as bait to catch other dragons, or maybe even cooked and eaten!

Heavy Metal, also known as Faith

Muzzle

YOU'D BETTER BE READY TO BATTLE A DRAGON!

There's only one thing to do when you're locked in a cell—start trying to break out!

TURN TO **75**

OR

There's no point in being free in an empty desert. Sit back and wait to see where this ride takes you.

TURN TO **98**

NINJA FACT!

Heavy Metal is a high-ranking Dragon Hunter until the ninja arrive in the First Realm. Her loyalties shift and she aids the ninja.

COLE ON A ROLL

As soon as Kai summons him, Cole skids onto the scene. His bike runs rings around Fire Fang, hemming it in while you and Kai launch missiles from the 4x4. But the weapons have no effect on this super-serpent, and before long you and the ninja are left with no choice but to retreat!

DATA FILE

COLE'S DIRT BIKE
» Built to traverse the Desert of Doom
» Emblazoned with Cole's elemental Earth symbol
» Equipped with shooters on both sides

BATTLE BIKE

Cole can pilot his dirt bike with just one hand while wielding his golden hammer weapon in the other. The all-terrain vehicle combines the speed of a bike with the steady tread of a tank, and is sized somewhere between the two.

NAS-S-S-TY NINJA!

Aspheera on Fire Fang

Pyro Slayer

Cole's Dirt Bike

Kai's Katana

YOU'RE GROUNDED!

Ninja training will get you so far, but sometimes you just need the right tool for the right job! On this occasion, ground forces are not enough to save the day—you need air support, too!

>> GO BACK AND TRY ANOTHER PATH!

BEHIND THE MASKS

The Royal Palace is not the safe haven you hoped it would be! Something has reduced most of the buildings to ruins, with only one small temple left intact. You go inside and find the royal Princess Harumi with two other Oni Masks. She is the leader of the Sons of Garmadon and is delighted that you have brought her the third mask, so that she can carry out her plan! Now what are you going to do?

THREE HEADS ARE BETTER THAN ONE!

You've unknowingly done your foes' work for them! The best thing you can do now is run for your life.

TURN TO **90**

OR

It's unlikely you can overcome the combined power of the Oni Masks. But you should still give it a try!

TURN TO **11**

ROYAL REVENGE

Princess Harumi is the adopted daughter of the Ninjago Emperor and Empress. She claims to be a fan of the ninja, but secretly blames them for the loss of her real parents when she was a child. Behind the scenes, Harumi has plotted her revenge against the ninja for many years.

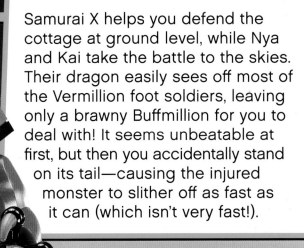

Samurai X helps you defend the cottage at ground level, while Nya and Kai take the battle to the skies. Their dragon easily sees off most of the Vermillion foot soldiers, leaving only a brawny Buffmillion for you to deal with! It seems unbeatable at first, but then you accidentally stand on its tail—causing the injured monster to slither off as fast as it can (which isn't very fast!).

Buffmillion

STRONG AND SILENT

Like all Vermillion Warriors, the Buffmillion is made up of hundreds of tiny snakes held together by psychic power. What sets the Buffmillion apart from its fellow soldiers is its immense size and strength—and the fact that it cannot speak, because it has four hissing snakes instead of a face!

Slackjaw

THE END OF THE TALE?

The simulation fades as fast as the Buffmillion, and you find yourself back with the real Nya. She says you clearly have all the bravery a ninja needs! But weren't you a bit curious to see who lived in the cottage?

>> CONGRATULATIONS! YOU HAVE COMPLETED YOUR NINJA MISSION!

SENDING OUT AN S.O.S.

As smaller pirate ships fly out to see who is approaching their sky base, you reach out and grab a sword from one of the pilots. You throw it toward the base and it clatters into one of its propellers, releasing a huge burst of energy. Reality starts to bend and warp around you, as you realize you have shattered the Sky Pirates' famous Sword of Souls and unleashed its awesome power!

SWORD OF SOULS

Also known as the Djinn Blade, the Sword of Souls is the most powerful weapon belonging to Nadakhan. The Sky Pirate captain uses it to trap his enemies inside a pocket dimension before feeding off their life force to increase his own abilities. If the sword claims enough unlucky victims, it can even reshape reality!

Sword of souls

New realms are appearing before you! Try to focus on the first one you see—a dry and dusty world.

TURN TO
14

OR

You've had enough of sand! Set your sights on the second realm you see—a land of ice and snow.

TURN TO
89

Kai takes you back to *Land Bounty*, the ninja's massive mobile base. Zane and the other ninja are there, planning their next move against Fire Fang. With your encouragement, they agree that their efforts so far are worthy of a party! Your mission for Master Wu can be put on pause … can't it?

DATA FILE

LAND BOUNTY

» Spinning shuriken weapons on both sides

» Deck-mounted cannon and fold-out missile launcher

» Quad bike launch bay between huge rear wheels

BREAKAWAY BASE

Land Bounty is a down-to-earth version of the ninja's flying base, *Destiny's Bounty*. But it has flying functions of its own. The entire upper level can break away to become a boatlike battle flyer!

IT'S BASICALLY A BEACH PARTY!

DISCO INFERNO

No sooner has your party playlist kicked in than Fire Fang launches a fresh attack. Now there's no hope for you or your mission as the city goes up in smoke! Seems like you partied too soon.

>> GO BACK AND TRY ANOTHER PATH!

NEST OF VIPERS

Your adventure begins in a steaming swamp, surrounded by giant eggs. Some have already hatched, while the nearest one is just cracking open! Peeking over the top of an egg, you see a slithering, snakelike creature keeping watch. You can't get away without her seeing you, but you don't want to hang around these eggs forever. What's best if you want to flee the nest?

HAPPY HATCH-DAY, LITTLE ONESSS!

RED ARMY

Giant eggs can mean only one thing—the Vermillion! These small red snakes mass together to become bigger creatures, such as Supreme Commander Machia and her army of Vermillion Warriors. These clever creatures are out to destroy anything that is not like them, and to do the dirty work of the Time Twins!

Make a run for it—and hope that your legs are faster than the snake guard's slither!

TURN TO 32

OR

Hide in one of the giant, empty eggshells for now and wait to see if the guard goes away.

TURN TO 7

NINJA FACT!

Most Vermillion Warriors wear helmets, but Machia likes to show off the snakes that grow from her head like hair!

Slab might not be at his best as a prisoner of the Dragon Hunters, but what he lacks in energy he makes up for in rage! When he realizes you are willing to battle him for the Hunters' amusement, he lets out a mighty breath that blasts you across the arena in a cloud of dust! As your vision clears, you see that you have landed in a jail cell on the other side of the base!

KEPT IN CAPTIVITY

The Dragon Hunters' base is equipped with all sorts of cells for different kinds of captives, but the biggest dragons are restrained with chains instead of cages.

MOCKED AND LOCKED UP

The Dragon Hunters laugh as they slam your cell door shut and lead poor Slab back to his own dungeon. They know they are going to have a lot of fun making you fight different dragons every day!

>> GO BACK AND TRY ANOTHER PATH!

ICE ON THE ROADS

You tell Zane that you saw one of the bikers hiding a mask in their bag as they left, and the ninja says there is no time to lose! The Master of Ice ditches his disguise as you both leap on bikes and race after the criminals. You soon catch up with them, and Zane freezes the road ahead, making everyone skid and the Oni Mask go flying! What will you do as the bikers flee without it?

DATA FILE

STREET RACER

» Silent running mode for covert operations

» Front section is a detachable drone

» Side blasters are built into the drone's wings

WATCH OUT FOR A SHARP FROST!

Oni Mask of Hatred

SNAKE BIKE

When Zane pretends to be Snake Jaguar, he has to prove himself to the biker gang by taking part in a dangerous road race. Nya provides him with just the bike to meet the challenge: one with artificial intelligence and anti-surveillance systems. It can get up to speed in seconds.

Forget that greasy gang! Grabbing the Oni Mask is the most important thing.

TURN TO **29**

OR

Leave the mask to Zane. Those bad-to-the-bone bikers can't be allowed to get away now!

TURN TO **20**

DRAGON OF DESTINY

Wu smiles when you make your request. He says you have proved your potential by seeking out the peace of the tea stall when chaos was raging all around you. You may have drawn his dragon here by accident, but every choice you have made so far has brought you to this moment—and now the dragon is sending all the ghouls scurrying back to where they came from!

WU'S WINGS

Master Wu keeps his own Elemental Creation Dragon a secret for some time, but eventually summons it to inspire Nya to become a fully fledged ninja. Once the creature is revealed, Wu calls on its powers again when he joins the battle against Morro and his Ghost Warriors.

READY FOR REALITY

A smiling Nya echoes Wu's words as your test comes to an end. She says that Master Wu is looking forward to meeting you in the real world, too, so that your training as a ninja can really begin!

>> CONGRATULATIONS! YOU HAVE COMPLETED YOUR NINJA MISSION!

As a passenger, you can only hold on tight and see where the pirates are eager to go. But when you spot their destination you wish you didn't know! You are fast approaching their huge flying base. If you end up inside it, you won't last long! This situation calls for drastic action—but what can you do?

DATA FILE

MISFORTUNE'S KEEP

» VTOL (vertical takeoff and landing) craft

» Armed with hidden cannons and disk shooters

» Built-in runway for launching smaller ships

SHIP AHOY, SKY DOGS!

Bucko

Grab whatever is at hand and throw it at the base. Hey, it's better than doing nothing!

TURN TO **53**

OR

Do absolutely nothing. It's the last thing the Sky Pirates will expect!

TURN TO **31**

FLYING FORTRESS

The pirates' flying fortress is a ship called *Misfortune's Keep*. Long ago it ruled the seas, but now it is an aircraft with engines that rotate so that it can take off and land like a helicopter. Although it has changed a lot, it still has a talking skeleton on the front who is happy to tell tales from the olden days!

When you finally fight your way through to Lloyd, you really wish you hadn't. This is not the Green Ninja as you know him, but the monstrous Morro, who has stolen Lloyd's form! Now you realize why there were so many ghosts around him. He wasn't fighting them—he was giving them orders! Now you are a prisoner of Morro and his minions, having walked right into their trap.

NINJA FACT!

Long ago, before he became a ghost, Morro was a pupil of Master Wu, who became the Elemental Master of Wind.

I'M MORE FIEND THAN FRIEND!

A DARKER SHADE OF GREEN

Unlucky Lloyd is possessed by Morro before he knows what is happening! Once he is under Morro's control he struggles hard to regain his freedom, but is in no condition to fight back. The other ninja do not get their familiar friend back until Morro has no more use for him.

Lloyd, possessed by Morro

A GHOST OF A CHANCE

As soon as you fall into Morro's clutches the simulation ends with an electronic sigh. Nya says not to blame yourself. You didn't know you would meet a possessed Green Ninja, so why not take the test again?

>> GO BACK AND TRY ANOTHER PATH!

BREWING UP WU

When you get to the tea stall, you see that its owner is another ghost! Before he can attack, you upend his cart and send his strange brew spilling everywhere. Tea leaves catch the wind and rise into the air. Seconds later, something much larger appears in the sky—it is Master Wu on his Elemental Dragon, which has been summoned by the smell of tea! How, asks Wu, can he help?

BUILD IT!

Give some other familiar city sights a spooky makeover with ghostly looking add-ons and creepy colored sections that look like slime!

TEA TO TRANSPORT YOU

When the Ghost Warriors descend on the City of Stiix, Wu is trying to live a quiet life. He is running his own tea shop in Ninjago City, where he sells all kinds of tea, from brews that are simply tasty to ones with special powers, such as Traveler's Tea. A cup of this can transport you from one place to another in the blink of an eye!

I PREFER MY TEA CHILLED TO THE BONE.

Ask Master Wu to help you prove your ninja worth right here and now in the City of Stiix.

TURN TO **58**

OR

Tell Wu you have seen enough of this spooky city, and ask him for a cup of Traveler's Tea!

TURN TO **112**

As you venture into the jungle, a rumbling sound overheard starts to get louder. You look up and see a terrifying flying machine made from what looks like rock and bone! Fortunately, the plane's pilot doesn't seem to have spotted you—they are chasing Skylor, the Elemental Master of Amber. Is there anything you can do to help her?

DATA FILE

'CONDRAI COPTER

» Part helicopter, part airplane!

» Wings fold up in attack formation

» Net trap flies out of snakelike "mouth"

DON'T MAKE ME GROUND YOU, SKYLOR!

Copilot, Eyezor

Pilot, Master Chen

LEAVE ME ALONE, DAD.

AMBER ALERT

Skylor becomes a friend of the ninja during the Tournament of Elements. She is the daughter of the villainous Master Chen, but takes after her brave and good-hearted mother, who was the Master of Amber before her.

If you can get the attention of the flying machine's pilot, it might just help Skylor to escape!

TURN TO **3**

OR

If you interfere, it could make things worse. Stay out of sight and let Skylor do her thing.

TURN TO **93**

AN ICY RECEPTION

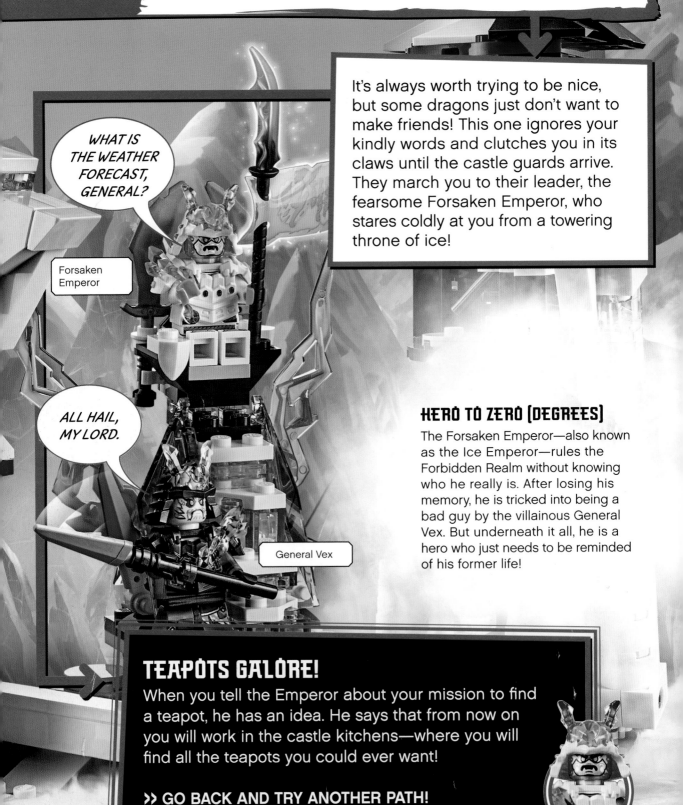

WHAT IS THE WEATHER FORECAST, GENERAL?

Forsaken Emperor

ALL HAIL, MY LORD.

General Vex

It's always worth trying to be nice, but some dragons just don't want to make friends! This one ignores your kindly words and clutches you in its claws until the castle guards arrive. They march you to their leader, the fearsome Forsaken Emperor, who stares coldly at you from a towering throne of ice!

HERO TO ZERO (DEGREES)

The Forsaken Emperor—also known as the Ice Emperor—rules the Forbidden Realm without knowing who he really is. After losing his memory, he is tricked into being a bad guy by the villainous General Vex. But underneath it all, he is a hero who just needs to be reminded of his former life!

TEAPOTS GALORE!

When you tell the Emperor about your mission to find a teapot, he has an idea. He says that from now on you will work in the castle kitchens—where you will find all the teapots you could ever want!

>> GO BACK AND TRY ANOTHER PATH!

GREEN FOR GO, GO, GO!

As you speed along with Lloyd, he says that the gang has stolen a dangerous Oni Mask for their leader, whose identity no one knows. When you spot a shortcut, Lloyd is able to get ahead of the bikers and bring them skidding to a halt. Now is your chance to confront the gang, but what are you going to say?

DATA FILE

NINJA NIGHTCRAWLER

» Rapid-fire cannons flip up in attack mode

» Giant gold blades shield cockpit sides

» Supercharged engine for extra power

MASKS TO RAID

Oni Masks are powerful relics from the First Realm, also known as the Realm of Oni and Dragons. There are three masks in total, and if the Sons of Garmadon can steal them all they will use them in a ritual that is sure to spell doom and destruction for Ninjago City!

INTERCEPTED? MORE LIKE, NINJA-CEPTED!

Tell them to hand over the Oni Mask or you and Lloyd will show them your Spinjitzu skills!

TURN TO **29**

OR

Demand that they take you to their mysterious leader, or ... well, the thing about Spinjitzu again!

TURN TO **69**

WU ARE YOU?

As you walk in the desert, you start to suspect that someone is watching you. You call out that you are a friend of the ninja, and a teenage warrior reveals himself. You realize it is Master Wu, but as he looked when he was much, much younger! He says he can help you find your way, but where exactly do you want to go?

SECOND CHILDHOOD

Wu arrives in the First Realm shortly after a time-twisting adventure that turned him back into a tiny baby! While trapped in this desert world, he quickly grows from a small boy into a teenager, before becoming his wise old self again—with a far more impressive beard!

DO YOU THINK I'D LOOK GOOD WITH A LONGER BEARD?

You know that there are dragons in this realm. Ask this young Wu to direct you to one.

TURN TO **108**

OR

If Wu is here, then surely so are the ninja. Ask him to take you to one or all of them.

TURN TO **34**

NINJA FACT!

Wu's aging process goes into reverse after he touches a powerful Time Blade. He only starts getting older once the effects wear off.

You leave the boat and chase after the retreating Vermillion, but run straight into their reinforcements! Before you have a chance to react, soldiers on scorpion-shaped racers surround you and seize your Time Blades. Now you wish you had gone back into the past, because your future looks suddenly bleak!

DATA FILE

VERMILLION RACER

» Pincerlike prongs for attack

» Central tire for tight turns

» Tall tail fin in rear, for balance

SCORPION TANK

Half-bike, half-tank, the Vermillion Racers are fast and formidable fighting machines. They are inspired by the shape of the stinging scorpion rather than the snake, but they are just as venomous as any serpent-shaped vehicle in the Vermillion fleet!

PICK YOUR BATTLES

When the simulation ends, Nya says that a ninja never tries to win the same battle twice! With the Vermillion already in retreat, you should have let them go and set your sights on an even bigger victory.

>> GO BACK AND TRY ANOTHER PATH!

AN ICE SURPRISE

BUILD IT!

Build a snowy mountain range by using gray and white bricks to make jagged, irregular shapes. Then add small transparent pieces to look like ice.

You're brave to battle the creature, but it only takes one hit from its swinging tail to catapult you out of the city and into another realm! With a flash of light, you find yourself beside a small ruin on an icy mountain. Two figures stand far apart in the distance. Which one should you head toward?

IS THERE ANYONE OUT THERE?

WINTER'S TALE

This wintry world is the Forbidden Realm. It is also known as the Never-Realm, as it's said that those that enter can never leave! The place was not always so frosty and forbidding, but has become colder and colder ever since an angry Ice Emperor made his home here. Now there is no summer in the Never-Realm at all!

The human figure—it looks like your friend, Lloyd the Green Ninja!

TURN TO **110**

OR

The large white wolf— something tells you it wants you to follow it!

TURN TO **6**

You turn your back on the base and set course for a safe place to muster your forces. But as soon as you start moving, you attract the attention of a Vermillion patrol! Swooping down on arrowhead hoverboards, they snatch the two Time Blades from your hands and use one to put you and your ninja pals on pause! Now there is nothing you can do as they take the superweapons for themselves!

RANK AND VILE

Slackjaw and Vermin are two of the Vermillion Army's countless soldiers. Each Vermillion soldier is made up of hundreds of tiny snakes, so can form and reform when damaged. Their army is constantly shifting up and down in number, making it hard to keep track of a pair of low-ranking soldiers like these.

THE GENERAL WILL BE IMPRESSED BY US!

Vermin

Slackjaw

PAUSE, REWIND, REPEAT

You are pleased to be un-paused as the simulation ends, but sorry not to have passed the test. Nya says you should try again and have faith in your friends, but never turn your back on the enemy!

>> GO BACK AND TRY ANOTHER PATH!

LOCKED UP WITH LLOYD

Given that you aren't a Spinjitzu master (yet!), you are relieved when the bikers agree to take you and Lloyd to their leader. You only wish you had been a bit more specific, because they take you there as prisoners, using Vengestone chains to suppress Lloyd's powers! Lloyd suggests that next time you should let him do the talking.

NO WORDS

The leader of the Sons of Garmadon uses "The Quiet One" as a code name. The Quiet One turns out to be Ninjago's Royal Princess Harumi. The story behind her secret identity can be traced back to her childhood, when the loss of her parents shocked her into a long-lasting period of silence.

Princess Harumi, in her "Quiet One" disguise

YOU'LL HAVE TO BE SMARTER THAN THAT TO OUTWIT ME!

NOT BAD FOR A BEGINNER!

Back in the simulation chamber, Nya is sympathetic. She says even though you ended the test in Harumi's jail, you did succeed in discovering that she is the gang's leader. And that's got to be worth another try!

>> GO BACK AND TRY ANOTHER PATH!

RIDER ON THE STORM

It takes the skills of a ninja to tame a dragon, but fortunately Stormbringer can sense you are not her enemy. She seems to understand when you say you would rather join forces than fight, and she flips you onto her back before breathing lightning in the direction of your captors! As they scatter, all you need to do is decide: where do you want to escape to?

REAL LIVE DRAGONS!

Unlike the Elemental Dragons that the ninja create by overcoming their fears, the dragons of the First Realm are real flesh and blood. The creatures still have elemental powers, however, and can form a bond with an Elemental Master.

Fly Stormbringer out of the arena, then take her to search the realm for Master Wu's missing teapot.

TURN TO 85

OR

Fly the dragon out of this realm altogether. There must be much nicer places to look for Wu's teapot!

TURN TO 45

NINJA FACT!

When the ninja visit the First Realm, Stormbringer becomes Jay the Lightning Ninja's dragon.

DAWN OF DOOM

You burst into the base just in time. The Vermillion and their leaders—the villainous Time Twins—are about to activate their ultimate weapon! The time-traveling machine known as Iron Doom will be their path to eternal power if it can't be stopped now. Is this the moment to use your Pause Time Blade?

DATA FILE

IRON DOOM

» This cyborg mech is a mix of circuits and snakes!

» The Time Twins control it with just their thoughts

» Weapons include giant swords and missile launchers

Acronix

Krux

Yes—use the blade to stop the villainous Time Twins and their monster mech in their tracks!

TURN TO **86**

OR

No—the power of a Time Blade is just what the Twins need to make their mech invincible!

TURN TO **26**

TIME-TRAVEL TERROR

Also known as the VTA (Vermillion Transport Armor), Iron Doom is designed to harness the power of the Time Blades. If all four blades are plugged into its chest, it will give the Time Twins the power to travel anywhere and any-when!

The Raid Zeppelin is no match for Jay's mighty dragon, and the creature holds the ship in its claws as you and Jay leap aboard and round up the crew. The Lightning Ninja leaves you in charge as you set course for Kryptarium Prison, where these scurvy Sky Pirates can be safely locked up!

KEPT IN THE KRYPT

Over the years, Kryptarium Prison has held some of Ninjago's most notorious villains, from Skulkin and Serpentine generals to the Sons of Garmadon gang and even Lord Garmadon himself. The Sky Pirates see a stint in prison as part of their job, and some spend more time in the cells than on board their ships!

IT'S VISITING TIME, PIRATES!

Doubloon

GREAT! CAN I VISIT THE BEACH?

Dogshank

SET COURSE TO FAIL!

Note to self: next time you take a pirate ship to a prison, be sure to lower its pirate flag! The moment you arrive at Kryptarium, you are surrounded by guards and locked up for being a pirate captain!

>> GO BACK AND TRY ANOTHER PATH!

DRAGON AT THE DOOR

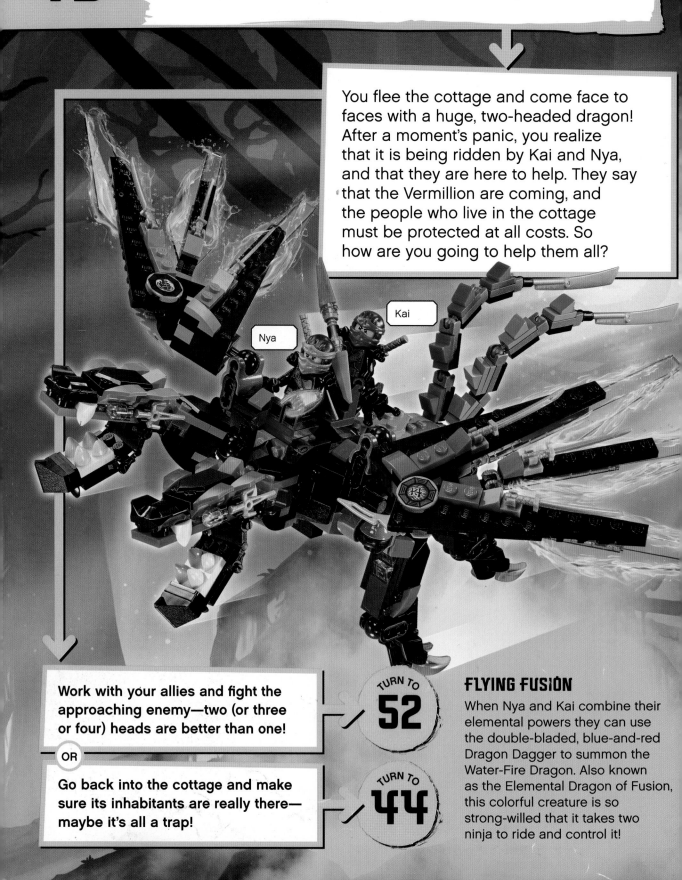

You flee the cottage and come face to faces with a huge, two-headed dragon! After a moment's panic, you realize that it is being ridden by Kai and Nya, and that they are here to help. They say that the Vermillion are coming, and the people who live in the cottage must be protected at all costs. So how are you going to help them all?

Nya

Kai

Work with your allies and fight the approaching enemy—two (or three or four) heads are better than one!

TURN TO **52**

OR

Go back into the cottage and make sure its inhabitants are really there— maybe it's all a trap!

TURN TO **44**

FLYING FUSION

When Nya and Kai combine their elemental powers they can use the double-bladed, blue-and-red Dragon Dagger to summon the Water-Fire Dragon. Also known as the Elemental Dragon of Fusion, this colorful creature is so strong-willed that it takes two ninja to ride and control it!

As you pluck up the courage to enter the Anacondrai temple, you see a fearsome-looking guard heading your way. You duck out of sight before he reaches you, and watch with interest as he checks on a prisoner in a shadowy cell. What will you do when he stomps off to continue his patrol?

GENERAL INFO

This is no ordinary guard! Zugu is the right-hand man of Master Chen—the leader of the Anacondrai worshippers. As a former sumo wrestler, Zugu is almost impossible to budge when he stands firm and all but unstoppable when he wants to move!

KEEP IT DOWN.

LET ME OUT!

Sneak a look through the bars of the cell. The prisoner inside could become an important ally!

TURN TO 48

OR

Stick to your plan of exploring the temple. The figure in the cell might give you away to the guard!

TURN TO 15

NINJA FACT!

Zugu once suggested Master Chen host "Sushi Sundays" for all his followers as a tasty treat. Chen said no!

THE HARD CELL

TANK TALK

The Dragon Hunters' Dieselnaut doesn't just have a detachable prison cell—the whole vehicle can split into two halves! Both sections are armed with missile launchers, and the back half has a crane arm for carrying captured dragons. With huge, go-anywhere tires and caterpillar tracks, this is one mean machine!

You struggle to break free, but the cell is sturdy and closely watched by a pair of guards. Your only other option is to make them set you free, so you start to be as annoying as possible. You tell them every detail of your adventures so far, and how the famous ninja really wouldn't be able to get by without you!

BUILD IT!

Make your own vehicles with breakaway sections. Use pieces that snap apart easily, such as clips and bars, or LEGO® Technic pins and bricks with holes.

Prison cell

FREE TO FAIL

Soon, the guards are so tired of hearing your tales that they eject the whole cell from their vehicle! It breaks open as it hits the ground, and you are free once more. Unfortunately, you are also totally lost!

≫ GO BACK AND TRY ANOTHER PATH!

Sadly, this Sky Pirate doesn't want any more friends! Before you even get a chance to say hello, she gathers you up in her massive arms and carries you off to an airship. She tosses you on board just as the craft starts to soar into the air. There is no way to escape from up here. Or is there?

DATA FILE

RAID ZEPPELIN

» Hot-air balloon, boat, and jet flyer all in one craft!

» Forward cannon mounted on scary dragon skull

» Trapdoor for dropping dynamite on enemies—or dropping enemies out!

MAN OF NOT MANY FACES

Pilot Doubloon used to pose as friendly and chatty, but was really a crook. When he tried to cheat the Sky Pirates, Nadakhan saw that he was two-faced and turned him into a pirate with a pair of permanent, unchanging masks!

Doubloon

Yes, there is. You could jump overboard and hope to land safely on the soft beach below!

TURN TO **103**

OR

No, there isn't. If you jump, you could land in the ocean! You'd better just sit tight for now.

TURN TO **59**

GUARDIAN OF THE GATES

You march boldly up to the castle gates, only to see a huge dragon swooping down to meet you! Like the castle itself—and everything else around you—it looks as if it is carved from ice, and would be painfully cold to touch. You must get past this creature if you want to enter the castle, but how will you go about it?

DEFENSE OF THE REALM

The Ice Emperor wields power equal to that of a ninja, and has conjured up his own Elemental Dragon to defend himself and his castle against attack. When inhabitants of the Forbidden Realm resist him, he sends the Ice Dragon to freeze them solid with its icy breath!

Use your red-hot fighting skills to make the monster melt away in fear.

TURN TO
113

OR

Employ your warm personality to thaw the chilling creature's heart with kindness.

TURN TO
63

When you enter the abandoned base you see that it is a blacksmith's forge, where weapons and armor are made. As Samurai X heads for the living quarters, you go for a closer look at the workshop. You pick up a sword from a weapons rack, and a very loud alarm goes off! The front door slams shut as the building goes into lockdown, and you realize you are trapped!

I SAID NOT TO TOUCH ANYTHING!

SECRETS OF THE SMITHY

Hidden deep in the swamplands, the building known as Dragon's Forge is where the Vermillion Warriors get their armor made. Every finished piece that leaves the forge is stamped with a special maker's mark, and—though the Vermillion do not know it—that mark is a secret message!

BY THE SWORD

With nowhere else to go, you find yourself back in the test chamber. Nya smiles and says you really shouldn't go around picking up strange weapons! Perhaps you should have stuck with Samurai X ...

>> GO BACK AND TRY ANOTHER PATH!

SMASH AND SLAB!

Slab is about to blast you with his sandy breath, but is surprised to see you aren't running away. Curious, he takes a closer look at you, and realizes that you share the same enemy. He tosses you onto his scaly back and uses all his energy to smash his way out of the arena. What will you do in the chaos that his dramatic exit creates?

KNOW YOUR HUNTERS

The leader of the Dragon Hunters is Iron Baron, who rules from a throne made of dragon bones. His second-in-command is Heavy Metal (also known as Faith), who eventually teams up with the ninja. Next in line are Jet Jack, who wears a jet pack, and Daddy No Legs, who has four robotic legs!

Slab has shown his strength. Stick with your new dragon friend as you make your escape together.

TURN TO
22

Slab

OR

Everyone's attention is on Slab. Slip off his back and sneak away into the desert during the confusion.

TURN TO
65

After completing a full loop of the castle's defenses, you arrive back at your trail of footprints in the snow. You wonder why you haven't seen any guards. Taking a closer look at the ground, you understand why. There are several other sets of footprints, and they're all following yours!

COLD WARRIORS

These guards, and the castle they defend, belong to the Ice Emperor who rules this realm. Led by the emperor's closest advisor—the devious General Vex—they call themselves the Blizzard Warriors and wield crossbows and ice katanas!

Blizzard Warrior

Blizzard Sword Master

FREEZE!

General Vex

SNOW WAY OUT

You turn around to see the castle's guards surrounding you. There's no escape from these cold-blooded warriors, who will happily leave you standing in the snow until you are frozen solid!

>> GO BACK AND TRY ANOTHER PATH!

HAUNTED HIGHWAY

Swerving along in Jay's awesome, ghost-catching car, you see people running in all directions. Some are coming from a road on the left, shouting about a huge, terrifying dragon. Others are running from the right, saying they've seen a spooky motorbike! Which way do you want Jay to turn?

DATA FILE

JAY WALKER ONE
» Gold-trimmed wheels and Lightning Ninja decals
» Adjustable ghost-catching cannon and cargo storage
» Cannon can also shoot elemental lightning!

WALKER'S WHEELS

The Jay Walker One is named after its current owner, but is also known as the Ghost Taker GT. This vehicle was built by the brilliant scientist Cyrus Borg. It is equipped with a ghost-catching cannon that sucks spooks into the clear blue containment unit at the back. No one knows quite how many ghosts it can hold at one time!

LET'S SNAG THOSE SPECTERS!

Left—a huge, terrifying dragon must surely be dealt with before a ghost bike!

TURN TO **4**

OR

Right—you've already tackled one dragon, but you've never seen a ghost ride a bike!

TURN TO **107**

BUILD IT!

Build a handheld box with a lid to create your own ghost trap. Put a warning on it so your friends are aware of its spooky contents!

As soon as you get close to the teapot, it reacts to the Traveler's Tea that is still sloshing around inside your stomach! It starts to give off a fierce glow, and all the Sky Pirates scatter in fear. When the ninja gather around to see what is happening, you try to explain that you have come from the future on a mission for Master Wu. But before you have a chance to say anything at all, everything disappears!

Master Wu's teapot

THE TASTE OF SUCCESS

After a moment of bright white nothingness, you find yourself back in the dojo with Master Wu. He is very pleased to have his teapot back, and to see you again! As you sit down to tell him about your adventures, you politely refuse another cup of tea …

>> CONGRATULATIONS! YOU HAVE COMPLETED
   YOUR NINJA MISSION!

TIPTOE INTO TROUBLE

Samurai X fires her grappling hook across the harbor. It lands on a tower at the entrance to the city, creating a tightrope across the water. On tiptoe, you take hundreds of tiny steps to reach the other side. You are relieved when you arrive, and amazed that no one spotted you. But then you realize why: a battle is raging between the ghosts and the ninja! How are you going to help?

CRYSTAL BRAWL

The Ghost Warriors take control of the City of Stiix when Morro uses a powerful Realm Crystal to release the ghosts from the Cursed Realm. The ninja fight hard to send them back where they came from, but the crystal just keeps bringing them back again—in greater and greater numbers!

Head for Kai the Fire Ninja, who is battling a host of ghosts in a blur of elemental energy!

TURN TO **106**

OR

Go after Jay the Lightning Ninja, who has been snatched by spooks and lifted off his feet!

TURN TO **21**

BUILD IT!

Stretch some string or thread between two LEGO builds to make a tightrope for a minifigure. Hook the minifigure on with a harness to turn it into a zip wire.

For all your efforts, you can't stop two of the missiles landing on the boat. But when you go to take a closer look, you see that they aren't missiles at all but a pair of powerful Time Blades! With the Vermillion still attacking the boat, you wonder: which blade should you use to get away?

POINTS OF INTEREST

The Time Blades were created long ago, when the Time Twins first threatened Ninjago Island. Once the Twins were defeated, Master Wu hurled the four blades into the Time Vortex to stop them from falling into the wrong hands. But eventually they came tumbling back into the ninja's modern lives!

Reversal Time Blade

Forward Time Blade

Use the green Forward Time Blade to jump ahead to a different adventure in your future.

TURN TO
112

OR

Use the orange Reversal Time Blade to make a different choice in your recent past.

TURN TO
55

NINJA FACT!

Each Time Blade is an armored glove (also called a gauntlet) that has absorbed a quarter of the elemental power of Time.

BATTLE STATIONS!

As you soar above the arena, you look down to see that the Dragon Hunters have quickly overcome their surprise at your escape! Every one of them is crewing the base's fearsome battle stations, and all of their weapons are pointed at you! There is no way they are going to let you get away, but with rockets going off all around you, it is too late to shift realms now!

CROSSING THE REALMS

The realms are 16 different locations that exist on different planes of reality. Ninjago is one such realm, and so is the First Realm. It is not easy to travel between the realms, but dragons can usually fly from one to another. There are also rare artifacts and forms of magic that act as passageways.

DON'T LET THEM GET AWAY!

Heavy Metal

THE NOT-SO-GREAT ESCAPE

In the face of overwhelming firepower, you have no choice but to surrender to the Dragon Hunters. As they lock you and Stormbringer away once again, you wish you'd taken a trip to a different realm!

>> GO BACK AND TRY ANOTHER PATH!

The Time Twins' eyes light up when you run at Iron Doom with the Pause Time Blade. This is just what they wanted! But when they see that you also have the Slow-Mo Time Blade, their triumphant looks turn to panic. Instead of using the blades on the mech, you use them on each other, causing time to go haywire! Iron Doom disappears into the Time Vortex, but so do you! Now what are you going to do?

MOVING WITH THE TIMES

The Time Vortex (also known as the Temporal Vortex) is a dangerous place where all of time exists at once. If you can navigate, it can be used as a path to the past or the future. But if you get lost, you can be trapped forever in an endless moment, while time moves on as normal for everyone else in the world.

Iron Doom is defeated so your work here is done. Travel forward in time to a brand new challenge.

TURN TO 112

OR

Disappearing in a time warp is not a ninja victory! Use the Time Vortex to turn time back so that these events never happened.

TURN TO 55

NINJA FACT!

Master Wu becomes lost in time after his own battle with Iron Doom, and ends up being turned back into a baby!

SPOOK ATTACK!

Ronin knows exactly where to find the ninja, and speeds off in their direction. But when you reach them, you see that they are under attack from a fearsome ghost dragon and a ghoulish gang of Skreemers! You know that you must act quickly to help your ninja friends— but how?

WELL, THIS IS A SCREAM!

Bow Master Soul Archer

A HOST OF GHOSTS

Don't believe in ghosts? Neither did the ninja, until Morro and his army of Ghost Warriors came to Ninjago! Now, with Morro on the loose, the team faces daily dealings with ghost dragons, ghost ninja, ghost vehicles, and ghostly green globs called Skreemers—which love to eat, screech, and land on people's heads!

Skreemers

Battle the ghost dragon with Ronin's R.E.X. The dragon may be big, but at least it is one-on-one!

TURN TO **18**

OR

Leap out of the R.E.X. to fight the Skreemers on the ground. There are lots of them, but they're only small!

TURN TO **38**

As you explore the outer edges of the tournament, you search for Master Wu's teapot. It takes a long time, and you are disappointed not to find what you are looking for. But you do eventually meet another ninja, Zane. He tells you that the tournament is over and the Anacondrai worshippers have been forced to flee! What will you do now?

I AM DETECTING NO SIGNS OF ANYTHING!

ZANE REBOOTED

When the Tournament of Elements begins, everyone thinks Zane the Ice Ninja has been destroyed. His ninja pals are delighted to find him alive and well, and together they put an end to Chen's phony tournament, which has been set up to trap them all.

Tell Zane why you missed all the excitement—maybe he can help with your mission.

TURN TO **95**

OR

Go with Zane to meet the victorious ninja team—you should go where they go!

TURN TO **105**

NINJA FACT!

Zane's shiny new look at the tournament shows his transformation from the Ice Ninja into the mighty Titanium Ninja!

SNOW BOUND

As you head for a soft landing in deep snow, you look down and see two separate figures crossing a mountainous landscape. One is a human who doesn't see your approach, while the other is a white wolf that watches you with interest. Once you are on the ground, you decide to chase after one of the figures—but which one?

SOMEPLACE NEVER

It is always winter in the Never-Realm (also known as the Forbidden Realm). The most distant of all the Sixteen Realms, it's also the hardest to escape from. A cold-hearted Ice Emperor rules the snowscape with his Blizzard Samurai, and has all but wiped out the peaceful beings that once lived beyond his Castle of Ice!

I MUST BE THE ONLY SOUL FOR MILES!

The human figure. From here, it looks like Lloyd the Green Ninja! He's a great leader to follow.

TURN TO
110

OR

The white wolf. The unusual way it looks at you suggests it is no ordinary animal.

TURN TO
6

When you turn to run, you find your way barred by the Sons of Garmadon! Princess Harumi orders them to take you to the temple dungeon, where you can't interfere with her revenge plans. With only a skeleton for company in your cold stone cell, you are forced to reflect that running away is never the answer!

SONS SET

All kinds of unusual characters make up the Sons of Garmadon. The only thing they have in common is a love of speed and bikes! Members include thrill-seeking Ultra Violet; mysterious Mr. E; best friends Chopper Maroon and Mohawk; and the giant general, Killow.

DO YOU THINK HE'LL SIGN MY SWORD?

THERE'S NO STOPPING LORD GARMADON'S RETURN NOW.

Mr. E

Chopper Maroon

Ultra Violet

SO NEAR, AND YET ...

You don't have to spend long in the cell before the simulation fades away. Nya says you came very close to passing the test. If only you hadn't doubted yourself after choosing to go to the Royal Palace!

>> GO BACK AND TRY ANOTHER PATH!

FRIEND OR FOE?

When your captors release Slab from his massive cage you can see he has not been well treated. You are sure that in battle you could dodge his attacks until he is exhausted and you are declared the winner. But you also think you might be able to make friends with the sad-looking creature. What should you do?

SLAB OF ICE

When the ninja find themselves in the Dragon Hunters' pit, Slab is not very welcoming and Zane, the Master of Ice has to use his elemental power to freeze him. But when they encounter him again he is far more friendly, using his own elemental power to team up with Cole, the Master of Earth.

It's better to go ahead with the contest. You don't have to hurt Slab and it will keep your captors happy.

TURN TO **56**

OR

It's worth trying to team up with Slab. Nobody else in this realm seems to be on your side!

TURN TO **79**

BUILD IT!

Build a simple battle arena by laying out loose bricks as a boundary. Or make something more ambitious with a scoreboard and spectator seating!

Nya waves goodbye as you speed off on her motorbike. Riding at top speed, you are able to explore the island in no time at all, and you realize it has no bridges, no ports, and no sign of Wu's missing teapot! In fact, the only thing you do find is a pair of Sky Pirates with a catapult—and they want to use you as target practice!

DATA FILE

MOBILE CATAPULT

» Huge wheels allow weapon to be hauled anywhere

» Pirates keep count of shots against dragons on the front

» Scary animal skull figurehead strikes fear into enemies!

LUDICROUS LANDLUBBERS

Before they became catapult cutthroats, Bucko and Sqiffy were just a pair of ordinary pals called Colin and Landon. But they wanted to be Sky Pirates, so Nadakhan gave the landlubbers the first two pirate names he could think of and reluctantly allowed them to join his crew!

Sqiffy

DON'T AIM THAT THING AT ME, SQIFFY!

Bucko

STRANDED!

Ninja bikes are cool, but they can't help you get off an island surrounded by water! By now, Nya will have left in the flyer, so all you can do is stick around and try not to get flattened by pirate projectiles!

>> GO BACK AND TRY ANOTHER PATH!

TUMBLE IN THE JUNGLE

When Skylor struggles to escape, you realize that hiding yourself was the wrong thing to do. You want to help, but now you are tangled up in the thick jungle greenery! Reaching out, you grab what seems to be an abandoned weapon to cut yourself free—but this only tips you into a trap set by the Anacondrai!

JADEBLADES

Long ago, bright green Jadeblades were used by mighty warriors from the original Anacondrai tribes. Years later, competitors in the Tournament of Elements race to find the blades, which Master Chen has hidden as part of his fiendish contest.

Jadeblade

HANDS OFF THE JADEBLADE!

Skylor

Krait

NO WAY OUT

There's no way out of the trap, so you can only wait until the Anacondrai worshippers come to claim you as their prisoner. If only you had come to Skylor's aid when you first had the chance!

>> GO BACK AND TRY ANOTHER PATH!

FIRE AND ICE

Kai has barely finished sending a signal to Zane when you hear the sound of Zane's ShuriCopter cutting through the air. You and Kai use the 4x4 to keep the mighty Fire Fang distracted while Zane rains down icy missiles to cool the creature's temper. The blazing beast does its best to fight back, but is finally forced to retreat. This is a victory to make the most of—but how?

DATA FILE

SHURICOPTER

» Rapid-fire six-shooters to port and starboard

» Landing wheels with built-in shuriken slicers

» Targeting display built into cockpit windscreen

FORBIDDEN FLYER

Zane's ShuriCopter is so named because of the spinning shuriken blades that defend it from attack on both sides. He flies the craft in the Forbidden Realm, after Aspheera sends him there using the power of Forbidden Spinjitzu.

COOL IT, FANG FACE!

Mount another assault on the creature as it slinks away from the city.

TURN TO **67**

OR

Let the defeated beast leave while you enjoy a celebration. There's no need to push your luck!

TURN TO **54**

DRAGON OF DECISION

You tell Zane about your mission to find Master Wu's teapot—and how you have had no luck finding it in this place and time. Zane agrees that you should continue your search elsewhere, and suggests you use his Titanium Dragon to take you to another realm. But where exactly do you want to go?

A DREAM COME TRUE

Zane first sees the Titanium Dragon in his dreams. When he accepts that he is now the Titanium Ninja (as well as the Ice Ninja), he gains the ability to summon the dragon for real. Zane uses the dragon to chase after Master Chen, who is on his way to destroy Ninjago City!

Take a ride to the First Realm— an ancient land of deserts and dragons.

OR

Fly into the Forbidden Realm— a land where secrets lurk amid the ice and snow.

TURN TO 14

TURN TO 89

BUILD IT!

Dragons come in all shapes and sizes. Try to build the biggest dragon you can, then try to make the smallest model that is still recognizably a dragon.

WATERWAY TO GO!

You bound onto Kai's boat before realizing that there is little room for passengers! Clinging on as best you can, you ask the Fire Ninja what you can do to help. He tells you that once he has steered the bikers away from trying to jump the canal, his work will be done and the rest of the mission will be in Lloyd's hands. The only thing for you to do is to keep holding tight and try not to get too wet!

DATA FILE

KATANA V11

» In speed mode, the vessel is an aquadynamic dart

» In battle mode, hidden missile-launchers emerge

» Long front section is used for weapons storage

I'M A LITTLE OUT OF MY ELEMENT...

FIRE ON WATER

Designed by Nya, Kai's Katana V11 is both a surface boat and a submarine. It boasts guided missile systems and sonar mapping equipment, and can even deploy depth charges. Nya has, of course, made it in her brother's favorite color: fire red!

JUST A DRY RUN

Kai's voice becomes Nya's as the virtual world fades and you find yourself back in the test chamber—and not at all wet! Nya says you've come too far to fail over one wrong choice, so why not try again ...

>> GO BACK AND TRY ANOTHER PATH!

GREEN GIANT

Master Wu's balloon swerves away from the island and leads you over the ocean to Lloyd. Lloyd isn't hard to find, as he is flying through the air on the biggest dragon you have ever seen! The dragon plucks you out of the balloon with its claws and flips you onto its back. Lloyd welcomes you aboard and asks if you're ready to face some Sky Pirates.

FLYING WITH FOCUS

Lloyd's Energy Dragon is an embodiment of his elemental power. It takes nearly all his concentration and willpower to bring the creature into being, so he only uses it for short amounts of time. If he were to lose his focus for even a second, the dragon would cease to exist!

Yes—as long as he's willing to go back and deal with the terrifying pirate you've already met.

TURN TO **19**

OR

Yes—so long as he's NOT going back to deal with the terrifying pirate you've already met!

TURN TO **37**

BUILD IT!

Why not build a spectacular perch for the dragon, in the color of its elemental power? The dragon can rest and recharge here between bursts of flight.

THIS PLACE IS A PIT!

It isn't long before the vehicle stops and you are led out of the cell into a vast base with a sunken battle pit. Your captors want to have some fun with you, and that means making you fight a dragon! They will let you pick your opponent, but which of two colossal creatures will you choose?

Iron Baron

... BEFORE IT CHEWS YOU!

CHOOSE YOUR OPPONENT ...

Arkade

Chew Toy

Stormbringer the Lightning Dragon looks angry but intelligent. Maybe you can reason with her?

TURN TO **70**

OR

Slab the Earth Dragon looks strong but slow. Maybe you can outrun him if you have to fight?

TURN TO **91**

ALL ABOUT THAT BASE

Known as Dead's End, the Dragon Hunters' base is a ramshackle settlement built from the limited resources of the First Realm. It is still a forbidding stronghold, however. The Dragon Hunters have complete control over who (or what) gets in or out—and who (or what) has to fight in the Dragon Pit!

PLAN X

Zane tells you where to meet Samurai X, and you roar away on a motorbike. You find her working on her magnificent mech, and give her the coded message straight away. It is a plan to defeat the Sons of Garmadon for good! Samurai X is eager to put it into practice as soon as possible. The only question is: where?

DATA FILE

SAMURAI MECH

» Built to replace the original red Samurai Mech

» Blasters on left wrist, spinning blade on right wrist

» Built-in jet pack allows it to fly as well as walk

WE'D BETTER GET STARTED.

The villains' own base is the place to strike. It's where they will be most off their guard!

TURN TO **120**

OR

The gang will know every inch of their own HQ. Better to take them on in the streets!

TURN TO **115**

VIRAL CONTENT

The ninja finally learn that Samurai X is their android pal P.I.X.A.L. after she and her mech are infected with a computer virus. When she recovers from the virus, Samurai X becomes a fully fledged member of the ninja team. Nya upgrades Samurai X's mech to make it more powerful than ever before!

With Lloyd at the controls, you take off toward the castle. But before you get there, you start to feel very odd! At first, you think it is airsickness, but then you see a bright, white glow on the ground. You realize that the Traveler's Tea in your tummy is reacting to the missing teapot, which is half buried in the snow beneath you! Lloyd glides toward the glow.

DATA FILE

TITAN MECH FLYER

» Twin shooters built into the narrow nose

» Storage for katana blades above each shooter

» Adjustable wings flip around to attach to mech

GIANT SHOULDERS

Lloyd's flyer is made from the back and shoulder sections of his Titan Mech. The mech can still act as a giant walking warrior without the flyer attached!

THAT'S A GREEN LIGHT FOR LANDING!

TEA FOR TEAMWORK

As you dig the teapot out of the snow, you start to thank Lloyd for his help. But in a flash you are back in the dojo with Wu. He has now been joined by the ninja, and it is Lloyd who thanks you for the adventure!

» CONGRATULATIONS! YOU HAVE COMPLETED YOUR NINJA MISSION!

TRICK OR TREAT

When you reach your destination, you are surprised to see that the supposed enemy base is in fact a simple cottage, and not at all scary looking! You go inside with Samurai X and find a freshly brewed pot of tea steaming away on a table. Maybe this place isn't so abandoned … in fact, maybe it isn't an enemy base after all! How will you find out the truth?

GOOD BREWS

Tea is a very popular drink in Ninjago, and at one point Master Wu even opened his own tea shop called Steep Wisdom. Some teas give the drinker special powers—such as the ability to travel between Realms or to grow an instant beard—but most are simply tasty and refreshing!

MY SENSORS ARE PICKING UP INCOMING FOOTSTEPS …

Wait and see who comes back for their tea—they might be friendly, and they might have cake, too!

TURN TO **44**

OR

Get out of the cottage while you still can—for all you know the Vermillion might like to drink tea, too!

TURN TO **73**

BUILD IT!

Make a colorful rug like the one in the cottage by building a wall of bricks in a symmetrical pattern and then laying it down flat.

Skylor helps you search the jungle, but you can't find any teapots at all! Instead, you come across Lloyd, the Green Ninja, speeding his way to the Tournament of Elements. You jump into his Jungle Raider so you can continue your quest at the big event. But should you make a grand entrance with Lloyd or sneak into the tournament on your own?

DATA FILE

JUNGLE RAIDER
» Long, golden katana swords for protection

» Side-mounted headlights for navigating dark jungle overgrowth

» Huge, spiked wheels for covering tricky terrain

THIS RAIDER IS AN AWESOME RIDER!

GOING GREEN

The Jungle Raider was originally a purple buggy used by the Anacondrai worshippers. During the Tournament of Elements, Lloyd uses his elemental power to turn it into a green-and-gold custom car that fits much better with his personal brand!

It's time to get to the heart of the action. Go with Lloyd all the way into the tournament.

TURN TO 27

OR

It's better to sneak in while all eyes are on Lloyd. Get him to drop you off at the edge of the event.

TURN TO 88

Jumping off the airship seems like a good idea—until you look over the edge and see how high up you are! Just as you decide to stay on board, the ship lurches to one side and you tumble overboard anyway! Luckily, Jay the Lightning Ninja is following the ship. When he sees you fall he speeds ahead and catches you on his dragon!

DRAGON BUNCH

When Nadakhan traps all the other ninja in a pocket dimension, Jay uses his Elemental Dragon to seek out recruits for a new team that could take on the Sky Pirates. This team of "Ninja Replacements" includes Dareth, the so-called Brown Ninja, and Skylor the Elemental Master of Amber.

I'M A REAL BOLT OUT OF THE BLUE!

Jay's Elemental Dragon

Thank Jay for saving your life—then ask him to take you back down to earth!

TURN TO **37**

OR

Encourage Jay to storm the ship—after thanking him for the rescue, of course!

TURN TO **72**

Looking down from the jet, you spot a jungle clearing. It is the location of one of the events in Master Chen's tournament. You ask Cole to land, and he agrees when you explain your mission for Wu. Just moments later, Cole is battling Chen's henchman Sleven over a fiery lava pit! Cole looks like he has it under control, but you can never trust a snake!

BUILD IT!

Master Chen's tournament takes place in themed battle arenas. Why not build your own arenas inspired by the different ninja's elemental powers?

SCARED SLEVEN

Like all of Master Chen's followers, Sleven believes that one day he will become a snakelike creature. He really doesn't like the idea, because he is secretly afraid of snakes! You'd never guess it from his purple snake tattoos and snake-skull helmet.

THE HEAT IS REALLY ON!

IF ONLY I WAS THE NINJA OF FIRE—OR ICE!

Cole

Sleven

Stay and watch the battle from the sidelines in case Cole needs your help.

TURN TO **17**

OR

You came here to find Wu's teapot, and that's what you're going to do! Cole will be fine on his own.

TURN TO **88**

PARTY PEACE

The ninja are thrilled when you join them for victory celebrations at their mobile base, the DB X. You enjoy the party atmosphere for a while before trying to turn the conversation to your mission for Master Wu. But each ninja you speak to thinks it sounds like a job for one of the others—or something to worry about tomorrow instead!

DATA FILE

NINJA DB X

» Six-wheeled all-terrain mobile headquarters

» Name stands for Destiny's Bounty Express

» Can be controlled by an auto-pilot robot!

Kai

Lloyd

Jay

BACK-UP VEHICLE

Nya built the DB X in case the ninja's ship, *Destiny's Bounty*, was ever out of action. During the Tournament of Elements, Master Chen steals the vehicle and uses it against the ninja, but Nya reclaims it for the team.

Cole

TURN IT UP, ROBO-DJ!

Nya

Zane

DISCO TECH

The ninja are all true heroes, but sometimes they can be a little too easily distracted! Master Wu might not like it, but for now all you can do is forget your quest and dance the night away in the DB X!

>> GO BACK AND TRY ANOTHER PATH!

Moving so fast that he is little more than a streak of red, Kai signals danger for his green-glowing enemies! Ghouls are flying left and right as the Fire Ninja does his thing, and you realize that he doesn't need your help at all. You can no longer see the other ninja you spotted before, so you must find another way to make yourself useful. What is the best thing to do?

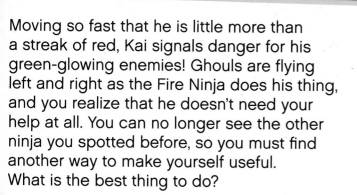

Chain Master Wrayth

Ghost Ninja Ming

With everybody else fighting, you should do something different. Take time out at a nearby tea stall to consider your next move.

TURN TO **61**

OR

With everybody else fighting, you should join in! Forget about tea and be like Kai by finding some ghosts of your own to battle!

TURN TO **38**

SUPER FLY KAI

Kai is the first ninja to master the long-lost martial art of Airjitzu. This allows him to lift off of the ground in a vortex of elemental energy. The result looks like a mini whirlwind, but is as powerful as a huge tornado! Kai and the other ninja use their new skill to defeat Morro and his ghost army.

ROAD WRAYTH

You swing right just in time to see a ghoulish green motorcycle disappearing around the corner. You urge your ninja companion to speed up, but on the next street you just miss the motorbike again! Only the eerie howl of its engine lets you know which way to go—almost as if it is deliberately leading you astray!

DATA FILE

CHAIN CYCLE

» Spiked wheels and sword-covered sides

» Ghostly "head" with red eyes and fangs

» Whipping "tail" serves as a catapult

MEAN MACHINE

The Chain Cycle is the property of Chain Master Wrayth, a spirit who used his ghostly powers to transform an ordinary motorbike into a monster! Wrayth is skilled in many martial arts, but his favorite weapon is a chain with a spectral scythe blade at one end. It can turn anyone it touches into a ghost!

GIVING UP THE GHOST

Suddenly, you find yourself back in the training room with Nya. She says the test is over. While you were on a wild ghost chase, the threat that you chose not to follow has laid waste to Simjago City!

» GO BACK AND TRY ANOTHER PATH!

When you promise not to reveal the location to anyone else, Master Wu leads you to the hidden nest of Firstbourne, the legendary "Mother of all Dragons." He tells her that you need her guidance, and then helps you climb onto her bright red back. As she rears up, ready to fly, it dawns on you that you can now search anywhere for the missing teapot. So where will you go first?

FIRST AMONG DRAGONS

All other dragons are descended from the mighty Firstbourne, who embodies all the elemental powers. Long ago, she and the First Spinjitzu Master tried to stop a battle that was raging in the First Realm. Now she spends her life trying to keep her children safe from deadly Dragon Hunters.

You will fly out of this realm altogether. You've got a bad feeling about this place!

TURN TO 45

OR

Search this realm thoroughly before you fly somewhere else. It can't be all desert, can it?

TURN TO 22

NINJA FACT!

As the son of the First Spinjitzu Master, Wu has been able to bond with Firstbourne, just like his father before him.

WRONG FOOT FORWARD

Everyone at the tournament is surprised to see you leap into the battle arena—especially Kai! He was just pretending to lose to Karlof, who is really on the ninja's side. The surprised Master of Fire tries to warn you that the dojo is full of Master Chen's traps, but it is too late. With a single wrong step, you activate a trapdoor in the floor and tumble into the fire pit below—taking poor Kai with you!

THE FLOOR IS THE FLAW IN THIS PLAN!

Kai

FIRE POWER

As the Elemental Master of Fire, Kai can make flames and fireballs with his bare hands, protect himself and others using fire shields, and control the spread of blazes that are already burning. He can even use flames to fly through the air!

PIT STOP

If you fall into a flaming pit, be sure to do it with a Fire Ninja! Kai's elemental power keeps you from getting cooked, but you're still in a hole and well and truly trapped! If only you'd listened to Lloyd …

>> GO BACK AND TRY ANOTHER PATH!

MOUNTAIN MECH

It is Lloyd the Green Ninja! He is pleased to meet a fellow adventurer amid the ice, and he leads you to a magnificent mech that can fly as well as walk. As you jump on board, he says he is heading for a mysterious castle but can't decide on the best way in. What do you think the two of you should do?

LET'S MECH A START!

DATA FILE

LLOYD'S TITAN MECH

» Wields a giant katana blade in its right hand

» Shuriken slicer on left arm doubles as a shield

» Upper section detaches for flight mode

March up to the front door of the castle and walk in like you own the place.

TURN TO **77**

— OR —

Fly the mech over the top of the castle and make a surprise entrance from above.

TURN TO **100**

LLOYD ALONE

When the ninja travel to the Forbidden Realm, Lloyd splits off from the others and takes his mech on a personal quest to find Zane, who is missing in the icy wasteland. While he is away, Nya takes charge of the rest of the team.

DJINN FOR THE WIN!

As you race into the thick of battle, you see the teapot start to glow. Realizing that it is reacting to the Traveler's Tea in your belly, you wonder if it could be the real thing after all! But before you can make a dash for it, you see Nadakhan, the captain of the Sky Pirates, swoop in and seize it for himself!

THERE'S POWER IN THAT POT!

Nadakhan

CAREFUL WHAT YOU WISH FOR

Nadakhan is no ordinary pirate captain. He is the last living djinn—a genielike being with the power to grant wishes. He enjoys twisting people's words so their dreams come true in extreme and unexpected ways. Once he has tricked someone and transformed their life, they have little choice but to join his crew!

TEAPOT OF TERROR

Oh no! This is exactly what Wu didn't want to happen! Now Nadakhan has the power to travel through time, there's no telling what havoc he will cause. If only you had kept focused on your mission!

>> GO BACK AND TRY ANOTHER PATH!

With a flash, you find yourself in a dark, indoor space. You feel confused, as if you've had a bit too much Traveler's Tea! But you don't have time to worry about that, as a light comes on and you see that you are in a grimy garage. A biker gang is preparing to ride out the door, leaving just one of their group behind. This must be your new mission! What should you do first?

GARMADON'S FANS

A biker gang called the Sons of Garmadon becomes a menace in Ninjago City at a time when Master Wu is missing and Lloyd is leading the ninja. The gang is devoted to the villainous Lord Garmadon, and hopes to bring him back to Ninjago Island from the Departed Realm!

FIRST ONE TO THE BIKES IS GARMADON'S BIGGEST FAN!

PREPARE TO BE BEATEN.

SMALL DOESN'T MEAN SLOW, YOU KNOW ...

Skip Vicious

Ultra Violet

Nails

Stick around and explore the strange garage, but only when the biker gang is out the door!

TURN TO **42**

OR

Sneak out with the bikers as they leave, to find out where you are and where the gang is going.

TURN TO **35**

BUILD IT!

The bikers' garage base is in a disused subway station. What other Ninjago City locations could you build, either in full working order or taken over by villains?

DRAGON'S EYE VIEW

Making yourself look as fierce as you can, you race at the Ice Dragon in an attempt to scare it away. When it flies up into the air, you think your plan has worked—until you notice it is taking you with it in its talons! As you soar helplessly in the sky, you fear you are done for, until you see a shining light in the snow. It is Master Wu's missing teapot, glowing with time-travel energy!

NINJA FACT!

Nya the Water Ninja destroys the Ice Dragon after learning to use her elemental power in a world where liquids are always frozen.

ELEMENTAL EMPEROR

So, just how is the Ice Emperor able to make his own Elemental Dragon? The answer is revealed when Lloyd confronts the Emperor and learns that he is really Zane! The Titanium Ninja has been led astray by Forbidden Spinjitzu, but Lloyd's friendship brings him back to his senses.

POT LUCK

The dragon is dazzled by the light and drops you right beside the teapot. As soon as you touch it, you are transported back to Master Wu's dojo, and he applauds your bravery (and your luck)!

>> CONGRATULATIONS! YOU HAVE COMPLETED YOUR NINJA MISSION!

You cling on tight behind Samurai X as she powers her speedboat across the harbor. The roar of the engine draws the attention of every Skreemer in the city, but the vessel is fast enough to dodge them. In fact, everything is going fine, until a glowing ghost ship appears from nowhere right in front of you! Samurai X says it might just be an illusion, but do you want to test that theory?

DATA FILE

SAMURAI X SPEEDBOAT

» Long, narrow shape for slicing effortlessly through water

» Water jets and blasters on both sides of the cockpit

» Detachable swords can be used in combat or to defend the back of the boat

Yes! Ignore the apparition and speed on toward the city as if the ghost ship isn't there.

TURN TO 38

OR

No! The ghost ship looks all too real to you. You need to slow down and prepare to fight.

TURN TO 47

MULTIPLES OF X

Samurai X is the name Nya sometimes uses before she becomes a ninja. She gives up the semi-secret identity during the ghostly goings-on in the City of Stiix, when she realizes she is destined to be the Master of Water. After Nya becomes the Water Ninja, the title of Samurai X passes to the team's android ally, P.I.X.A.L.

HERE COMES THE CHOPPER

The city streets are the bikers' natural home, and when you confront them here, you don't get a chance to put your plan into action! Even with the help of Samurai X, you can't hope to defeat this well-oiled fighting force—especially when it is led by the giant General Killow on his awesome Oni Chopper!

DATA FILE

ONI CHOPPER

» Custom-built for Killow's incredible bulk

» Front wheel is a tire-shredding saw blade

» Flip-out side blades for running enemies off the road

MR. BIG

Some think Killow is the leader of the Sons of Garmadon, but he is actually second-in-command to the real ringleader, "The Quiet One." When Killow wears the orange Oni Mask of Deception he is able to move things with his mind as well as his massive muscles!

END OF THE ROAD

Nya's friendly face replaces Killow's gruesome Oni Mask as the street scene fades away. She says you came so close to completing your mission that she won't let you give up now. You must have one more try!

>> GO BACK AND TRY ANOTHER PATH!

Jay's mighty blue mech bounds through the jungle in huge leaps. You have to cling on extra tight to keep from falling! It's hard to tell where you're going, but eventually the tropical greenery starts to thin out. As you hear the distant sound of combat, you realize you are about to arrive at the Tournament of Elements! Is it time to get off the mech?

DATA FILE

ELECTROMECH

» Left hand has two built-in blasters

» Right hand can wield an ancient Jadeblade

» Originally a "gift" from Master Chen

THERE IS ONLY ONE SEAT—HANG ON TIGHT!

WALKER'S WALKER

Jay Walker is the only one of the ninja not to have his own mech before the Tournament of Elements. A leg injury forces him to use the ElectroMech to get around Master Chen's island, and he likes it enough to keep it once his leg is healed.

Yes—ask Jay to drop you off at the edge of the tournament, so you can explore from the edges.

TURN TO **88**

OR

No—stick with Jay until he gets to the heart of the event, so you can explore from the center.

TURN TO **27**

BASE INSTINCTS

With time moving more slowly for the Vermillion, the ninja easily evade their slack attack. Leaving the boat behind, you join Lloyd and Kai as they follow the sluggish snakes' tracks back to their base, where plenty more Vermillion soldiers are busy preparing for something big. Could this be the perfect time to strike?

Vermin

BATTLE SSSSTATIONS, SSSERPENTS!

Tannin

DROPPING IN FOR A BITE

The Vermillion's fortress base is hidden deep in the swamps and also serves as the Time Twins' headquarters. Though it looks like a simple structure, it is peppered with pitfalls for unwary intruders. Chief among these are the snakes that slither over every surface, looking for foes to sink their fangs into!

Slackjaw

Yes! With two brave ninja at your side, you should storm the base now and not wait around!

OR

No! You need even more ninja to take on this threat. Back off until the rest of the team arrives.

TURN TO 71

TURN TO 68

BUILD IT!

Make your own scary LEGO snakes by linking moving parts (e.g. hinge bricks and ball-and-socket connectors) in a wiggly, wavy line.

THROWING SHADE

It doesn't take long for Zane to stomp onto the scene in his gleaming white Titan Mech. Wielding two titanium blades, he launches straight into a sword fight with the Ghost Mech, while you and Cole use the Blaster Bike to trip up its mighty feet. The Ghost Mech tumbles down the mountain, shattering into pieces. This is a ninja victory to be proud of. Let the celebrations begin!

DATA FILE

TITAN MECH
» Pilot wears spook-proof Deepstone armor
» "Head" section provides extra cockpit protection
» Blasters mounted on either side of pilot's seat

TITAN UP

The Titan Mech is Zane's first ever walker! It's also the last mech standing after the other ninja's walkers are destroyed. Upgraded by Dr. Cyrus Borg to include Deepstone cannons for fending off ghosts, it even boasts a rocket-booster backpack for following phantoms into the air!

SO LONG, SPOOK!

A SPIRITED PERFORMANCE

The ninja have gathered around to watch you take the test in real life. When they witness you defeat the Ghost Mech, they are convinced by your ninja skills and welcome you onto their team!

» CONGRATULATIONS! YOU HAVE COMPLETED YOUR NINJA MISSION!

SO CLOSE TO STIIX

You land at the edge of the City of Stiix, on one of the small islands that dot its busy harbor. You are surprised to see Samurai X keeping watch, until she warns you that the city has been overrun by ghosts! You make it your mission to find out more. But how will you make it past the ghoulish guards on patrol?

LIFE IN THE CITY

Stiix is a ramshackle city on stilts in the Endless Sea. Its isolation makes it a perfect base for pirates and petty crooks, as well as for villains such as Morro and his Ghost Warriors. When Morro makes the city his base, many citizens are turned into ghosts and the buildings themselves become one giant monster!

Travel with Samurai X in her speedboat. It is fast, but the guards might hear its noisy engine.

TURN TO **114**

OR

Use a grapple gun to approach silently by tightrope. It will take longer, though, so you might be seen.

TURN TO **83**

Zane's undercover investigations have revealed that the gang's leader has a base in ... the city's Royal Palace! It is up to you and Samurai X to get inside, and when you do, you learn that the bikers' boss is none other than a Royal Princess! With her gang out hunting for more Oni Masks she is utterly undefended and no match for you and your new friend's mech. Now her dastardly plans will never be fulfilled!

QUIET LIFE

Ninjago's Royal Princess Harumi lives a secret life as leader of the Sons of Garmadon. She sneaks out of the palace in simple clothes to recruit crooks for her gang, and promises them great rewards if they do her bidding. To them, she is simply known as "The Quiet One."

SWEET SURRENDER

As soon as the Princess surrenders to you and Samurai X, the simulation is over. You look around the training room to see that Nya has been joined by the whole ninja team—who all look very impressed! Nya says you have saved Simjago and passed the test. You are now ready to walk the path of a ninja!

» CONGRATULATIONS! YOU HAVE COMPLETED YOUR NINJA MISSION!

Penguin Random House

Project Editor Beth Davies
US Editor Megan Douglass
Senior Designer Anna Formanek
Designer James McKeag
Pre-Production Producer Siu Yin Chan
Senior Producer Lloyd Robertson
Managing Editor Paula Regan
Managing Art Editor Jo Connor
Publisher Julie Ferris
Art Director Lisa Lanzarini

DK would like to thank: Randi Sørensen,
Heidi K. Jensen, Paul Hansford, and Martin
Leighton Lindhardt at the LEGO Group; Selina
Wood for editorial assistance; and Julia March
for proofreading.

First American Edition, 2020
Published in the United States by DK Publishing
1450 Broadway, Suite 801, New York, NY 10018

Page design Copyright ©2020
Dorling Kindersley Limited
DK, a Division of Penguin Random House LLC
20 21 22 23 24 10 9 8 7 6 5 4 3 2 1
001–315808–Apr/2020

A catalog record for this book is
available from the Library of Congress.
ISBN 978-1-4654-8955-5
ISBN 978-1-4654-9214-2 (library edition)

Printed and bound in China

A WORLD OF IDEAS:
SEE ALL THERE IS TO KNOW

www.dk.com

www.LEGO.com